GAME ON

An Ozzie Novak Thriller

Book 2

By
John W. Mefford

GAME ON
Copyright © 2017 by John W. Mefford
All rights reserved.

V1.0

Sugar Hill Publishing

ISBN: 978-1709372-96-4

Interior book design by
Bob Houston eBook Formatting

To stay updated on John's latest releases, visit:
JohnWMefford.com

One

A battle between my senses of sight and smell raged mightily in my brain. Off to the side of a small apartment building sat a rusted, dilapidated swing set. It was on the verge of being devoured by weeds and vines. In fact, the vines had wrenched the metal into a pretzel-like configuration.

An intake of breath brought with it an aroma that, on its own, would normally move you to a place of harmony and peace. The sweet scent of bougainvillea, plumeria, and orchid was both organically intoxicating and—because of this odd sense of dread that had clawed at me since I'd landed at the airport—toxic.

I lifted part of the lei that hung around my neck—full of vibrant pinks, reds, whites—and asked myself why I hadn't left it in the minivan. The sweet smell was over the top. Or maybe the odor had crossed into the pungent zone because of my body composition. My stomach churned like that of a little kid who'd overdosed on Halloween candy.

Indeed, the sensory overkill had done a number on me. As a person with a hearing impairment, that wasn't too surprising. I relied upon my four other senses as if I were clinging to a float in the middle of the ocean. An ocean as big as the Pacific, which, according to street signs, sat about fifty miles to the east of Fern

Forest, a small, forgettable community set inland on the Big Island of Hawaii. Or as the countless travel guides had called it on the plane ride over from Austin—the Orchid Isle.

I put my hand on a rickety wood railing to cross a muddy moat, and my fingertip felt the prick of a nail. I wiped the hint of blood on my jeans.

"Smart one, Ozzie. Add 'Get a tetanus shot' to your list of fun-filled activities on your first trip to Hawaii," I muttered to myself.

Just then, a woman slammed a door on one of the downstairs apartments. She trekked through weeds with an open purse tucked under her arm. I held out a hand, prepared to ask if she knew Denise Emerson, but it was obvious she wanted no part of me. Her sunken eyes stayed on her direct path. She wore a hairnet and a brown dress uniform that said she worked at a diner. She brushed against my shoulder without a word, then slipped behind the wheel of an ancient sedan and drove off.

Why anyone would choose to live in this place was a mystery. Then again, as I walked across the small bridge and contemplated the upheaval I'd experienced in the last week or so, perhaps they were just unlucky in life, going through a period of time when one bad thing built on top of the next.

A breath clicked in the back of my throat as a sobering fact took hold of my thoughts.

Your daughter—a person you didn't know existed until about twenty-four hours ago—may very well live in this wondrous dwelling.

I stopped at the edge of the U-shaped complex, looking for an indication of which apartment might be "Unit E." From where I stood, I saw nothing on the doors. I raked my fingers through my hair, which normally had a bit of a wave to it. In the salty, humid air, the ends had begun to roll into curls. Poppy, a bartender friend of mine back home, would, at about this time, smack the counter and ask me, "Love your hair, Oz. You want me to make you a Shirley Temple?" She loved to razz me. I would then quickly point out that she looked like a member of a reggae band from Mars—she of the red dreadlocks pinned behind her head.

Enough screwing around. I pulled the folded letter from my pocket and verified the address. "Unit E" was written in the upper left-hand corner of the envelope. I popped the letter against my opposite hand, contemplating the letter's authenticity. From what I could recall, ten years earlier, Denise seemed like a straight-up person. We'd dated briefly toward the end of our senior year in high school. She was fun, happy, the life of the party. I never got the sense she would be the kind to screw with someone's life just for the hell of it.

But again, that was ten years ago. Under normal circumstances, most people go through at least two metamorphic stages between eighteen and twenty-eight. And as of right now, nothing about this felt normal.

My thoughts flipped to the key part of Denise's letter. *I'm sorry I never told you, Ozzie, but you have a daughter. And she's in danger.*

That had ignited an action on my part that some might say was a desperate attempt to flee all of the drama back in Austin. Some of those same people might also point out that such an action was counter to my training as a lawyer—to first logically walk through the theoretical permutations on why Denise would send me this letter now, ten years after the fact.

Danger.

The word had prompted my nearly instantaneous response to travel to Hawaii; it was one of those trigger words for me. But there was an additional draw that had pulled me to the Big Island. The very real possibility that I might actually have a living relative.

My adoptive family had raised me since I was an infant. While it was a dysfunctional family—and still was in many ways—I'd never really put much thought into finding parents who'd tossed me into the expendable bucket. Their loss, my gain, I figured.

You don't even know her name, Oz.

Oh, yeah—there's that part. For whatever reason, Denise, or possibly someone posing as her, had forgotten to mention my daughter's name. That had limited my ability to verify that this daughter of mine existed at all. Was that because of the urgency or emotion of the moment when Denise, or perhaps her proxy, had penned this letter? Or could it have been by design?

That's right, I was actually going there. A nefarious plot to lure me out of the moderate chill—not meant as a euphemism of my current relationship status with my wife, Nicole—of Austin, Texas, so that I could be screwed over by some bizarre scam in one of the most popular travel destinations on Earth.

But here I was. Two thousand miles later. And while this section of Fern Forest could have been a rundown corner on the east side of I-35 in Austin, I recognized the contradictory irony of crisscrossing words like *nefarious* and *scam* with the paradise of Hawaii.

Ah, the games that your mind will play when sitting on a charter airplane for eight-plus hours with wall-to-wall college kids who clearly couldn't go for long without taking a shot of something over eighty proof.

I circled the rim of the inside of the first-floor apartments. No sign of "Unit E." Hell, no sign of human life. I toddled up to the second floor, where the sidewalk dipped toward the railing. I paused and eyed each window from the top of the steps, trying to get a bead on whether there were any inhabitants in this place. All I could see were plastic blinds and doors with tic-tac-toe games etched on them.

I wiped a drop of sweat off my forehead; then I glanced to the courtyard below. Was there any way that one of my old lawyer buddies, maybe someone from the old firm, could have played a trick on me? Wouldn't that be the ultimate prank? Tell a guy with no blood family that he has a long-lost daughter in some exotic paradise, one who was in grave danger, nonetheless.

Okay, I added the "grave" part. Still, though, it worked with the plot.

But, if for some bizarre reason, someone had pulled off one of the greatest pranks in modern history, provoking me to impulsively jump on the next flight to Hawaii, then the real fool would be them. I'd check out the apartments just to make sure there was no sign of Denise or a daughter who looked anything like me. Then I'd jump back into my minivan and head for the nearest all-inclusive resort and start the rejuvenation process.

I could already taste the Knob Creek on the rocks.

With a little extra energy in my step—I stayed as far from the railing as possible—I ambled down the walkway, stopping every few feet to cup a hand against a window. No sign of life anywhere. I wondered momentarily if the woman I'd seen earlier had the whole place to herself.

I completed one leg of the U; then I turned left. At the first door, I noticed something different. The letter "G" was carved into the door. I leaned backward while glancing left and counted down two more doors.

The adrenaline rush was so fast and unexpected, I felt like the base of my skull had been zapped.

The door was open, just a crack. My other sense, that sixth one, had been pinged.

Two

Given my lack of quality hearing, I instinctively put my head on a swivel and started to shuffle close to the partially open door. The last thing I wanted was not to hear someone coming up behind me. Despite the absence of life in this place, I wasn't about to take any chances.

I made it to the door, and sure enough, I found an "E" carved on it, although it was waist high. I dipped my head and peeked through the crack. It was dark, but I could just make out a kitchen table with books and papers on top.

Another glance behind me. All clear.

I knocked twice. "Anyone home?"

I waited a few seconds, but no one responded. I tried the same routine again and waited even longer this time.

All was quiet. Too quiet.

I nudged open the door and took a single step into the apartment. My eyes went straight to the green, wooden kitchen table in front of me. Coloring books covered it, some of them open to reveal the colored images. These weren't little-kid coloring books, for sure. The person had used colored pencils to embellish the detailed designs. One was a beautiful depiction of a waterfall cascading off a breathtaking cliff.

"Hello?" I was at a disadvantage. If someone were calling out in a soft voice from another room, I probably wouldn't hear them. I walked through a living room with furniture that didn't match and found a single bedroom. An unmade queen bed, the smell of perfume in the air, but no people. The hall bathroom had makeup, a hair dryer, and hair-care products. No people, and no real sign that a kid lived here.

Except for the coloring books, and even that was a stretch. An adult with aspirations of learning the art of drawing could have created those pictures. I spun on my sandals and headed back to the kitchen.

A chair was toppled over. Not sure how I missed that a minute ago. My eyes picked up red marks on the drab linoleum. I lowered to my knees and ran my fingers across the floor. Under the table, I spotted some colored pencils that had been smashed into tiny pieces, as if a heavy shoe had crushed them.

I tried to swallow, but my throat had gone dry.

On the other side of the table near the wall, I found an envelope on the floor. I crawled over and picked it up.

It was addressed to Denise Emerson. *So she does live here.* Unless this was a different Denise Emerson than the one who was my prom date.

My pulse ticked faster.

I eyed the front door. People don't leave their doors open like that—not unless they were in a huge rush.

She's in danger, the letter had said. Had Denise actually been referencing herself, thinking that if she mentioned a daughter, I was more likely to come than if it were just her? Given the dreadful condition of the complex, her life had taken a wrong turn somewhere.

Again, *if* it was her.

Pictures. She had to have photographs around here somewhere. I probably missed them in the one bedroom.

I quickly pushed up to head back to the bedroom.

Footfalls peppered the walkway. With no weapons on me, I plucked a dirty skillet off the stovetop and held it above my head. The door popped open.

"Ozzie!"

It was Denise. Makeup snaked down her face, but I could never mistake her eyes, the same icy blue. She looked worn, and her hair was a different color, but it was her.

"What's going on, Denise? Did you write me this letter?" I whipped it from my pocket and waved it at her.

Tears sprung from her eyes, and before I could take another breath, she barreled into me with open arms.

"They have her, Ozzie. They took our daughter." She fought through the sobs, then looked me in the eye. "They have our Mackenzie."

Three

My heart sank. I set down the skillet, slowly inhaled and exhaled, and then gently took Denise by the arms.

"Tell me what's going on, please."

She gasped a few times, as if she were having a difficult time getting words out. I found a cup on the kitchen counter and poured her some water. As she chugged the water, I ripped a paper towel from a roll and gave it to her. She wiped her face and got her breathing under control.

I gave her a minute. "You feeling better?"

"Thank you." Her voice was raspy, as if she'd been yelling.

"Start from the top. Where is…Mackenzie?" The name sounded strange coming off my lips.

"It's the *yakuza*. They took her from me."

I was a master at reading lips. That had always helped me piece together words I didn't quite hear. I wondered if I'd heard her correctly. "*Yakuza*—the Japanese crime syndicate?"

She nodded repeatedly. "Yes, it's them. You've got to help me get her back. Please. She's all I've got, Ozzie. Will you help me?" She was firing off words so fast it was hard to keep up, each phrase more animated than the last.

"Of course I'll help. I'm here, aren't I?"

A breath, and then she dialed back the intensity a couple of notches. "You are." Her eyes scanned me from head to toe. "You got my letter."

"You must have mailed the letter a week ago or so?"

"I'm worried about her, Oz. Mackenzie is..." She raised a jittery hand and wiped a tear from her face. I noticed her fingernails were down to the nubs. She'd ignored my question, or she'd been too rocked by the situation to listen clearly.

"I'm just trying to take this all in. I'm a lawyer—"

"Of course you are. Wow. Just like your dad."

I offered a tight-lipped smile. We could talk about Dad and everything else that had transpired over the last decade once we got Mackenzie back. "I need to understand the timetable, okay?"

"Okay. Right. Makes sense. What did you ask me?"

"You sent a letter. You must have been worried for a while. When did you send it?"

"About a week ago."

"Okay, when was she taken?"

"After she got home from school."

"Today?"

"Yes, today. Do you see why I'm so worried?"

She should be worried regardless, but I saw this as a small positive. "Better today than a week ago. So, have they communicated with you at all? Asked about a ransom, or said what it would take to get her back safely?"

"No, nothing."

I looked off and found a framed picture above the couch. It was a painting of a black-sand beach with steep cliffs in the background. Seagulls flew overhead at dusk as waves crashed into rock formations. It had to be a knock-off of a print.

I turned back to Denise, her glassy blue eyes as clear as the ocean water. "The door was open when I got here. Why?"

"I ran out of here when I came home early and found that she'd been kidnapped. The door is a piece of crap and doesn't shut well unless you really play with the lock. I didn't have time to screw with it."

"Where did you go?"

"Back to the school, about four blocks down. Sometimes she goes back there and plays with friends."

"You don't think she's at a friend's house?"

She held up her cell phone. "I called the parents of her four best friends. No one has seen her after they walked home together."

I felt a trickle of sweat bubble off my sideburn. I used my shoulder to wipe it off. "This *yakuza* angle. I have my doubts, but it—"

She pounded her shoe into the floor. I then realized she had on heels and was wearing a navy-blue pantsuit with a blue-and-white polka-dot silk shirt. Outside of her smeared makeup and frizzed-out hair that was a combination of red, brown, and blond, she looked almost professional. She didn't match anything else about this place.

"You don't fucking believe me," she said, taking a step back.

"No, Denise, that's not it. Look, I used the wrong word. I don't doubt you. I'm just wondering why the *yakuza* would bother to kidnap your...our daughter."

She put a hand to her face, but it didn't stop the new surge of tears. "I fucked up, Ozzie. And I think it might cost Mackenzie's life."

Four

There was something about Denise that seemed off, other than the obvious. I couldn't pinpoint it exactly. Perhaps I was being influenced by this ghetto-like apartment.

"Look," I said. "Nothing you could have done justifies kidnapping a child. Nothing. So get that out of your head."

I wasn't sure she believed me, but she gave me a single nod.

"Okay, let's just call the police and get their resources on this."

"Are you kidding me?" She pushed me in the chest, although she was the one who went backward a step. She probably weighed less than half of my two hundred ten pounds.

"What? What did I say that was wrong?"

"You haven't listened to me," she said, poking herself in the chest. It was so violent I felt certain she was bruising herself. I tried not to stare at her chest, which in the past might have been an issue. Now, not so much.

"Denise, I'm here for you…for Mackenzie. Which is why we need to call the cops." I pulled out my phone. Before my thumb could punch the nine, she slapped the phone out of my hand.

"What the hell are you doing?" I bent down and picked up my device. Scowling, I looked it over. The screen wasn't cracked, but there was no telling if any internal damage had been done.

"You can't call the cops." She smacked one hand into the other three times. "They'll kill her, Oz." A gasp, as she put a hand to her face and fought back more emotion. "Do you hear me? They will kill my precious little Mackenzie."

Her voice seemed to echo—I wasn't sure if that was my hearing aid or an actual reverberation. Her sobs ceased, and there was a moment of silence. We just stood there and looked at each other. For the first time since she'd walked through the door, her face, while blotchy, gave no indication of what she was thinking. Me? I had no clue which way to take this or how to fix it, how to bring back a girl I didn't know, a girl who had my blood in her veins.

At least a minute passed, and as I stared into her eyes, my mind couldn't help but shoot back to prom night, when I'd borrowed my father's Cadillac, walked up to the door of her home, and rang the doorbell. Her mom had answered, and, before I could ask if Denise was ready, she swung back, and there her daughter stood. The lighting hit her just perfectly. She looked angelic. My heart had kicked into another gear, and I'd just gawked at her like boys at that age are prone to do. I remember not being able even to speak. She wasn't just beautiful, though. She had this graceful confidence about her, as if I were about to take the arm of a princess. It had sounded cheesy running through my head even as I was thinking it, but that didn't negate the butterflies fluttering in my stomach. Was it love? It was difficult to pinpoint, actually. Lust, certainly. But, for one night, we'd connected on a level I'd never experienced before that moment, as if we had this perfectly aligned energy. We ended the night in a hotel room, making love. That must have been when Mackenzie was conceived. The next morning, with birds tweeting and the sun peeking through the trees, I had kissed her goodbye. A week later, we graduated and, like most high school couples, knew it was time to move on, to experience college without trying to juggle a long-distance relationship. I think she was headed out of state, but I really couldn't recall.

She sniffled, and I let out a sigh.

"Why didn't you tell me?" I asked.

"I..." Her eyes momentarily found the floor; then she looked at me, her lips pressed together. "I was just confused. I didn't know what to think. I found out when I was here, in Hawaii."

I tilted my head.

"I visited my aunt and uncle here on the Big Island. It was all part of a big graduation present. I planned on staying here a month. But that's when I found out I was pregnant. I struggled with what to do, whether to call you, or whether to even have the baby. I couldn't make the decision, and then the next thing I know, my aunt is taking me to the doctor, and I'm hearing the heartbeat. I connected with her at that moment."

"Wow. Sounds powerful."

"You don't have kids?"

I followed her gaze to my left hand. I was still wearing my wedding band. I twisted it on my hand, feeling a bit awkward. "No kids for me."

Her mouth opened, but no words were spoken.

Then I replayed what I'd said. "I'm sorry. I just meant that I have no kids with my... Well, I guess she's still my wife."

Something crossed her face, just for a split second. It was the smallest hint of the girl I'd taken to prom. Maybe she thought there was something there for us to rekindle. My stomach felt like it was trying to push its way into the back of my throat. I had so many emotions and thoughts waging an internal battle.

"You know I can't just sit here and not do anything to find Mackenzie."

"That's why I reached out to you, Ozzie. You always seemed like you had a good head on your shoulders, like no moment was too big for you."

I wasn't sure whether to thank her or be pissed at her for not telling me about my daughter. Again, the competing emotions. The knot in my stomach only grew larger.

"But that was when I was just scared. Now, they've taken her. I don't know what to do. But the *yakuza* has people everywhere, including the police department. That's a known fact on this island."

An idea, one that might not go anywhere, came to mind.

"I need to make a call."

She reached out and touched my arm.

"It's okay. I'm not calling the cops."

Not on the island, anyway.

Five

I kept my promise, although Denise wouldn't stop chattering about the potential risk we were taking through the entire two-hour drive over to the east side of the island, essentially retracing the path I'd taken earlier when I'd flown into Kona. We were on our way to meet a retired police officer from the Hawaii County Police Department.

A new friend of mine, Detective Brook Pressler with the Austin PD, had taken my call on the first ring. Within minutes, she'd pulled in her pal from San Antonio, Detective Stan Radowski. Stan and I had met earlier when I almost took a case for his friend. Long story. Anyway, Stan had just returned from taking a dream vacation with his wife to the Big Island. Cops, I learned, were like geese. They flocked together, or sniffed each other out, even if they were on vacation or retired. Apparently, Stan and his wife Bev had met a colorful former Hawaii police officer while here, and they'd hit it off.

Stan made a call and got back to me. His contact would meet with us, but we had to go to him.

"You're still not grasping the reach of the *yakuza*," Denise said.

I wiped my face, a bit tired of hearing how unfamiliar I was with crime, even organized crime. I'd studied plenty about it during my law-school days at Georgetown and had even done some side-reading once I'd passed the bar. I had to admit, though, that my knowledge of the Japanese mafia was limited at best. But what made her think she was the preeminent source?

"You never told me why you think the *yakuza* took Mackenzie," I said, glancing at her in the passenger seat.

Just then, she slammed her foot into the floorboard. "Look out!"

I whipped my head around to see the back side of an eighteen-wheeler almost on top of us—we were closing in on him at the speed of light. I punched my foot into the brake. The minivan swerved; the brakes squealed like I'd just run over a pig. I checked the speedometer. We were still at seventy, zipping down the east side of a mountain, actually the dormant peak of Mauna Kea.

Denise shrieked as I gripped the steering wheel with everything I had. The back end of the minivan pulled left and then right. I took my foot off the brake for just a second. We increased speed, but the vehicle righted itself. We were clear of the truck but still moving fast. I tapped the brake again. The car vibrated, slowing only ever so slightly. I could smell burning rubber.

"Is this how it's all going to end?" she yelled, her back pressed into the seat.

I ignored her. My eyes caught a curve at the bottom of the hill. At this rate of speed, we'd plow right through the median. If we didn't hit another car going in the opposite direction, we'd probably go airborne over the side of the cliff.

I couldn't jam on the brakes. They might completely give. I had to be patient...in the span of about twenty seconds. I gently applied pressure. At the hint of a squeak, I lifted my foot.

"What are you doing?"

"Trying to live to make our meeting with the cop," I said, my voice strained. I went through the same process—braking just a bit, then lifting my foot—four times in the next few seconds. When the speed dipped below fifty and we were close enough to see the angle of the curve, I took a breath. The road flattened out, and I pulled off to the side of the road and stopped the car.

"Brakes need to cool," she said, before I put it in park.

I used my T-shirt, which portrayed a Johnny Cash concert at Folsom Prison decades ago, to wipe sweat from my face.

"You still have a six-pack?" She snorted.

I glanced down, realizing I'd been exposing my belly. "Eh."

"Do you still swim every day?"

"Not every day. But it helps me relax."

"Cool." She looked toward the side of the road. Wispy clouds clung to the top of the mountain. Straight ahead, off in the distance, the sun shimmered off the ocean. It seemed too picturesque for words.

"Let's find Mackenzie; then, hopefully, you can have one of your relaxing swims in the ocean."

I nodded. "That would be cool." The eighteen-wheeler we'd passed zoomed by us, rocking the minivan. "Hey." I put my hand on top of hers for a second until she looked at me. "How are you connected to the *yakuza*? Why would they want to take your child?"

She searched my eyes and then said, "Because I threatened to go to the chief investigator from the Attorney General's Office— that's why."

"For what? Did you have something on them?"

Her jaw jutted out, and then she nodded. "The last ten years…" She looked away again, shaking her head. "The last ten years have been tough, Ozzie. My aunt and uncle both passed away, and I was left to take care of Mackenzie on my own."

I wanted to ask why she didn't come back to the States and reach out to me, but she didn't need me peppering her with more questions.

"I've been through a rough time, Oz." A deep, long sigh. "I have demons in me that, if they come out, I turn into a different person."

It was beginning to sound like I'd been sucked into a predictable horror flick. But I knew this was no joke. This was her life, or what was left of it. "And?"

"Ever heard of Ice?"

I shook my head.

"It's crystal meth. You smoke it. Hawaii has been a breeding ground for that shit since the '80s. Well…" She paused again as tears welled in her eyes. "I turned to prostitution to make ends meet. I experimented with Ice and got hooked. Bad."

I knew where this was headed, why her guilt was eating her up. Where there was heavy drug trade, organized crime was usually very close by.

"And Mackenzie?"

She shut her eyes for a moment, took in a deep breath. "She watched me crumble. I wasn't there for her. I wasn't always a good mom. Sometimes, I'd wake up, strung out, not know where I was. Then I'd find my way home, and she'd be there, coloring, or already in bed. She's an amazing little girl."

Tears streamed down her face, but she wasn't breaking down. Maybe she had a line that she wouldn't cross, or couldn't cross, when it came to her addictive past and breaking down about it. It was a different story with her daughter, of course. She had broken down plenty already. "I've been sober for almost three years now."

"That's great, Denise. You should feel proud." It didn't sound right, those words, since her addiction had brought this *yakuza* group into her life.

"So, if you didn't have a relapse, how did it happen? Was it some type of drug debt they're trying to collect?"

She pushed her chin out again. I thought she was about to go off on me. She swallowed, then said in a controlled manner, "The drug world is behind me. Like I said, I've been sober for almost three years. I went to junior college, got my associate's degree. I worked as a waitress most of that time, which paid the bills. Barely. But we got by, and I stayed clean. We were happy. And then I got my dream job."

She paused.

"Where? Doing what?"

"Accounting."

"So you're a numbers person."

"Who would have thought it, right? Certainly not our trig teacher, Dr. Copley." A brief smile. "I got a job at this real-estate development company, Palm Tree Dreams."

Sounded like it could have been a brothel, but I kept my strange thoughts to myself. "How long have you been working there?"

"About three months, which was long enough to see something weird going on in their books."

"Like?"

"It's rather complex to describe, but essentially, I believed they were laundering money."

I started the car and put it in drive. "And what did you do with this information?"

"I went to my boss and told him. He acted like he didn't believe me, so then I showed him."

"How so?"

"There are basically three stages of money laundering: the placement of the dirty money, the layering of said cash, and the integration of the cash. It's rather involved, but I found a trail."

"Did you convince him?"

"Reluctantly, he agreed. But I didn't think he'd do anything about it, so I said if he didn't share this with someone he trusted higher up in the company or someone from the board, then I'd be forced to go to the Attorney General's Office."

Her story sounded like one of those movies set on the East Coast, maybe Boston or Brooklyn. But I wasn't naïve. The tentacles of organized crime were everywhere. "Was your boss connected to the *yakuza?*"

"I didn't think so. But I got a cryptic email a couple of days later that warned me if I went to the Attorney General's Office, then they would hurt me or my daughter."

"Did you do it? Did you turn them in?"

She shook her head. "I never made the call."

Those words hung in the air the rest of our trip to the Four Seasons resort.

Six

Sipping on a frozen drink with a wedge of orange stuck to the lip of the glass, Keo Iwalani seemed to be enjoying the moment. He'd just walked off the eighteenth green at the famous Hualalai Golf Course. It was a Jack Nicklaus-designed course, according to the dozen or so placards on our way through the Four Seasons resort over to the clubhouse. The clubhouse, unlike any I'd visited on the mainland, was mostly outdoors. We sat in the shade near an open-air bar as a nice breeze cooled us off. An infinity pool was just below us, the pristine golf course surrounding our setting, and the majestic waters of the Pacific glowing from the setting sun.

"Thank you for coming all the way over here," Keo said before slurping in another mouthful. "You sure you don't want something else to drink?"

I glanced at Denise. We'd both gone with ice water. "We're good, thanks," I said.

Keo wore reflector sunglasses and a wide-brim hat. He looked like a tourist, a very wealthy one at that. I wondered how a retired officer could afford to not only play this course, but even get through the front gate. For now, I stayed focused on the task of trying to learn how we could get Mackenzie back.

"How long have you known the Radowskis?" he asked.

"I worked with Stan just briefly a few months ago. Met his wife at a small concert, but that didn't end up well."

Keo, who couldn't have been more than five-six, which would be eight inches shorter than my height, sat up straight in his chair. "You were there at the Belmont bombing in Austin?"

I nodded. Denise turned to look at me, but I stayed focused on Keo.

He said, "I just read an online story that said they have a suspect in the bombing and that he'll likely be charged." He waited a moment, but I didn't respond. "And it said the motive for the bombing might not be connected with terrorism after all."

He had no idea of my virtual proximity to the person he was discussing, an egomaniacal prick named Calvin Drake who'd essentially brainwashed my wife into providing the would-be bombers access to the concert venue. But the last thing I wanted to do was rehash that painful chapter of my life.

I flipped the conversation. "Stan said you still had connections."

"After thirty-four years on the force, you'd hope so." He smiled, took another pull on his drink.

Neither Denise nor I smiled back.

He set a hand on his knee and rubbed his face. He looked like he had a thin five-o'clock shadow, although this one was salt and pepper. "I need to know everything about this abduction."

Denise started in with her story. Not half a minute later, Keo set the palm of his hand on the table. "You must keep your voice down." He turned his head slightly as if he were looking for eavesdroppers. I had no idea exactly who or what he was looking at since his eyes were hidden behind his shades. "The people you speak of," he continued, "they have ears everywhere."

Denise gave me a knowing glance, then continued sharing her story. With light background music and the din of bar activity around us, I had to watch her lips to pick up what she said. I wanted to ensure this version matched what she'd told me. Was I having trust issues? And was it because of what she'd shared about her addiction to Ice, which, she admitted, had led to poor decisions with Mackenzie? A lot had changed in ten years, and that included my experiences as an attorney—where abuses, self-inflicted and otherwise, had made twenty-year-old girls and guys look like someone thirty years older and where lies or "variations of the truth" were just a part of a normal day. I just knew I couldn't take any chances.

Denise recounted the same information she'd told me. Amazingly, she kept her emotions in check, only once needing to wipe a tear from her cheek. My eyes volleyed between her and Keo, but it was impossible to get a read on a guy whose eyes were invisible.

He rubbed his stubbly chin after she finished. "Hmm."

"How can we find my baby? I can't go on much longer without having her with me. We've been a team for the last nine-plus years. Please, can you help me?" Now she was starting to lose her grip on her emotions.

I reached over and placed my hand on her arm. She looked at my hand. I thought for a second she might swat it away, but then she put her hand on mine.

I turned to the retired cop. "Keo, as you can see, we're in a tough spot. Calling in the police is an option, but Denise doesn't think that's wise."

"No, no, no," he said, waving his hand. "No cops. Too many ears. You did the right thing coming to me."

I waited as he stared at something over my head. He was thinking, contemplating our next move. But after more than a few seconds, I was pulled to look over my shoulder. A flat screen was showing highlights of an NHL game. What the hell? I turned back around and did my best not to rip into his lack of attentiveness. I opened my mouth, but he spoke first.

"I've always wanted to ice skate. I'm amazed at what these NHL guys can do with a stick and puck while someone is assaulting them."

I traded a glance with Denise. I could see her eyes narrow as crow's feet became more visible at the edges. She didn't think he understood the gravity of the situation. I could see her chest lift— she was about to explode.

"Hey, Keo," I said quickly, getting his attention before she went off on the guy.

He turned his head in my direction, but I couldn't be sure he was actually looking at me.

"Can you give us—"

"This is how I think." He pointed over my shoulder toward the TV. "Many locals stare at the ocean. They think it has all the answers. I've been surrounded by the water my whole life. Don't get me wrong, I love the water, the tropical fish. I love the dormant volcanoes, the black lava fields, the twenty-five-degree drop in temperature when I travel up to Waimea. But I find that I think best when watching sports. Hockey, football, baseball, basketball…just about anything other than UFC boxing."

Denise brought the glass of water to her lips, paused, and then gulped. She wiped her mouth with the back of her hand and puffed out a breath as if she'd just swum a hundred meters against a strong current. Every step of this process was painful for her. While I'd never met Mackenzie, Denise had obviously developed a connection with her that was sealed by more than just blood relation. Any relationship that survived addiction and all the fallout connected to it was one that was worth fighting for. Denise had battled a tremendous foe—a battle that might sit at the edge of her thoughts from now until her last days. But those days in between would be meaningless unless she was able to share them with Mackenzie.

My eyes were back on Keo. "Have you watched enough sports to feed your thoughts?"

He nodded and pulled a phone from his pocket. He appeared to be searching his contacts—he paused briefly and asked a passing waiter for his tab. Then he returned to his phone, mumbling something I couldn't decipher.

"Looking for someone who might give us some information?" I asked.

He nodded but kept moving his lips. He looked like a savant counting numbers. Out of the corner of my eye, I could see Denise grab a spoon and squeeze the handle until her knuckles went white. The pot was nearing its boiling point again.

I cleared my throat, hoping he'd be able to read Denise's rising anxiety.

The waiter approached, placed the check on the table, and walked away. Without looking—again, I couldn't verify it with certainty because of his too-cool sunglasses—Keo signed the receipt. He looked toward the ceiling as he leaned back in his chair.

"The Green Dragon," he said with a satisfying smile, as if he'd just won a poker hand. He lifted from his seat.

I looked at Denise, then at Keo. I was certain I couldn't hide my confusion. He sounded as if he were talking about some type of ancient god. Was this spirit going to magically give us the answers we needed?

"Let's go," he said, nudging his head toward the parking lot.

"To where?"

"The Green Dragon—where else?"

The Green Dragon was a place. Unconvinced this would be our point of enlightenment, I followed Keo through the resort and out to the employee parking lot.

"We're over here," I pointed over my shoulder.

"It's best if you ride with me anyway."

I shrugged, and we followed him to his car, a high-end Lexus sedan. When the doors shut, the car cooled off in about ten seconds. "Keo, what's up with the million-dollar lifestyle? You're a retired cop, not a retired Wall Street hedge-fund manager."

He'd just put the car in reverse, but he paused for a second. "On the island, nothing is more important than relationships. That's how I was able to hold my own as a detective for so many years, and it's continued in retirement."

Sounded fine, but it wasn't really an answer. He drove us up to the security booth. "Hi, Myron. How's your son doing after having his appendix removed?"

The chunky guard leaned out his window. "Couldn't be better. He's already itching to be on that surfboard again. I guess we'll see you tomorrow, Keo."

"You know it. I've got to keep an eye on the bad guys while I'm tearing up the course."

They waved at each other, and Keo pressed the gas. I just shook my head. "So you kiss ass to get all of this?"

"I run security for the visitors who have asked for the white-glove treatment. It's not a rough job, but I get to play one of the best courses in the hemisphere."

I gave a long nod as we wound our way through the entrance out to the main highway, nothing but postcard landscaping as far as the eye could see. "The car come with it?"

"Oh, this old thing?" He snickered. "Okay, it's not so old. But it's a loaner. Well, by now I'd call it a gift from a car dealer on Maui. I helped his daughter locate her husband. He thinks he owes me. You see, Ozzie, this is how the island does business."

Bartering. It was as old as any society in the world. But it appeared that Keo had perfected it. I just hoped he'd deliver the goods for us once we reached the Green Dragon.

Seven

Up a set of wooden stairs that creaked with every step, we made our way into the Green Dragon. With its expansive porch complete with a pair of rocking chairs, black shutters, and a screen door, the dwelling could have doubled as a South Carolina plantation home.

Instead, we walked into a high-end restaurant with aromas full of sweet spices. Their menu was considered Asian Fusion, and my olfactory sense picked up about twenty different smells.

The hostess, who wore a black, body-hugging, silk dress, lowered her head as if she were honoring our presence, then asked, "Would Mr. Iwalani enjoy his normal table?"

He brought a hand to his face, leaned in closer, and whispered something to her.

"This way, please," she said with a voice so soothing I would have followed her anywhere. She led us to a small side room. It had glass doors and was adorned with various sculptures of…green dragons. "She'll be with you in just a moment. Thank you." The girl bowed while closing the door, leaving the three of us alone.

"So I guess you know the owner or manager of this fine establishment?" I asked Keo, who, I noticed, was still wearing his sunglasses.

"The Green Dragon." He scratched his eye behind his glasses. I wasn't sure why he felt the need to keep up the cool act. But he'd distracted me.

"I'm sorry? We're at the Green Dragon. It's rather obvious," I said.

The doors opened before he could respond. In walked a woman closer to Keo's age. Her floral-covered dress flowed behind her, making it seem like she was gliding just above the floor. The apparent old friends gave respectful kisses on each other's cheek.

"*This* is the Green Dragon," Keo said, extending an arm in her direction.

She flicked a wrist toward Keo, offering a playful roll of the eyes. "Oh, Keo, don't play that game with your new friends."

We shook hands. When she did the same with Denise, she didn't let go. "I see trouble in your eyes." She glanced at Keo. "This is why you're here."

He nodded, then walked over to shut the glass doors. "Her daughter has been kidnapped by the Y-clan."

I tilted my head.

"Oh," he said, noticing my puzzled gaze, "that's our shared term for the *yakuza*. We don't like speaking of the most dangerous organized crime outfit in the world." His voice seemed to linger on the last word. "But…and this is something both Hulama and I will agree on…most of the time, those of us who do not fall under the thumb of the Y-clan have learned to coexist with them. It may not be a proper arrangement, but it is one that works for this society on the islands."

"Hulama," I repeated while looking at her.

"I'm sorry. Keo loves to play games with the Green Dragon discussion, harking back to the old days. My full name is Hulama

Kelii. My family is from Oahu, although I've been on this island for a good twenty years."

Denise reset her feet, put a hand on her hip. "I just can't keep playing this game, Keo. You're telling us that we have to fucking coexist with a crime syndicate. These monsters stole my little girl from me." She took in a shaky breath, wiped a tear from her eye. I moved a little closer, brushing against her arm. I didn't try to jump in and make excuses for Keo. It was up to him to show us how he could help. Otherwise, we might have to look at other alternatives, including getting the authorities involved.

"I apologize," he said, approaching us. "What I said was ill-timed at best. If it was up to me, all people would learn to coexist, to accept each other for their differences, to appreciate our diversity. I wish our country could find this happy place."

Denise put her hand over her face, her head and shoulders bouncing from a quiet cry. Keo wasn't helping.

Without warning, he removed his glasses from his head. One eye was shut. A pinkish scar ran vertically above and below that eye. "Denise, I know the brutality of the *yakuza* firsthand."

She sniffled, lifted her head.

He used his fingers to open his eye lid. All I could see were bloody ligaments. There was no eyeball. Denise gasped.

"This is what they did to me right after I watched them kill my partner. I know their brutality. But I also know their code."

Denise's tears dried up. I took hold of her hand. She squeezed my fingers.

"I brought you here to visit with Hulama because of her experiences with the Y-clan. She…" He paused, traded a glance with her. She nodded once and then put a hand on Keo's arm.

"I was known as the Green Dragon, back when I was a madam. I ran a house of prostitution."

Now our space got real quiet.

"I know what you must be thinking. My girls were offering a service and were paid top dollar. But some of the girls couldn't help themselves. They seemed to be magnets to the underbelly of society. And with that, they brushed shoulders with some bad people. Some of the henchmen with the Y-clan."

Denise took her hand back and momentarily chewed on a nail.

"I eventually shut down that business, but during that time, I got to know people." Her eyes snuck a gaze toward Keo. "People on both sides of the law. Then I opened this restaurant."

I quickly wondered if her contacts were too far out of the loop to do us much good.

A few seconds passed, and everyone looked at each other. I wasn't sure where to take it, so I made a random comment. "I like the concept," I said, looking at one of the dragon motifs.

Hulama didn't acknowledge me. "I also spend a fair amount of my time as a personal tour guide, to show people all the wonderful things this island has to offer. It's really the least I can do for our people."

"That's nice of you to give back," I said.

"Don't get me wrong. I'm paid quite well. But that's because my clientele are the uber rich. Some come from Japan. And a few of those I know are with the Y-clan."

Now I was starting to understand why Keo had brought us here.

"Do you think you can help us locate Mackenzie?"

She held my gaze for a moment. "What a beautiful name...Mackenzie," she said. "Do you have a picture?"

Denise pulled out her phone, swiped a thumb across the screen. She brought up a picture of a girl who could have been on the cover of a Disney brochure. As she handed the phone over, I walked to Hulama's side and continued staring at the photo. The girl had kinky hair, a rusty dirty-blond. Her blue eyes sparkled so much they appeared to be digitally enhanced. Her head was tilted just a bit, and through her playful smile, I saw a hint of mischievousness.

"She's a beautiful girl. Full of life." Hulama began to hand the phone back to Denise. "Do you mind?" I asked Denise. She nodded, and I took the phone and studied the girl who was purportedly my daughter.

Ever since I'd received the letter from Denise, I'd blindly accepted the fact that Mackenzie was indeed my daughter. I was never offered definitive proof, nor had I asked for it. Over the last few hours, whether it was because of my lawyer background or simply a natural desire to get to the truth, pangs of doubt had crept into my conscious thoughts. But now, looking into this nine-year-old girl's eyes, I thought I saw part of myself in her. It was beyond surreal. My chest tightened as I sucked in a deep breath.

I was her father.

Or was I seeing something that wasn't there at all?

Your hesitation to trust what you see is warranted, Ozzie. You've never looked into the eyes of anyone and seen yourself. No sister or brother. No Mom or Dad.

I could feel a lump in my throat. For the first time I could recall, I actually felt something about my real parents. Resentment maybe. Curiosity. An emptiness…actually, more like a void. My mom and dad—the ones who'd raised me—had been all I'd known. They had shaped my values, taken care of me, made me feel safe and loved, at least in their own way. But I would imagine most families had a similar makeup, in that they were all unique in how they interacted and showed love to each other. Sure, we were dysfunctional. But show me a family or any relationship that didn't have a few edges that weren't frayed.

Case in point: my marriage to Nicole, or what was left of it after her dalliance with a maniacal killer.

My eyes refocused on the phone.

"That's our daughter, Ozzie," Denise said, leaning against my shoulder.

I turned my head and looked at Denise. Her eyes were moist.

"Mackenzie. I really do have a daughter," I said, texting the picture to my phone.

She rested her head against my chest. After a second passed, I put my arm around her and kissed the top her head.

Was this the family I was supposed to have all along? Surely, if I'd been by Denise's side, she would have taken a different path, steered clear of drugs and all the demons associated with it. But another thought hit me: I was thinking like the Ozzie of today, not an eighteen-year-old kid.

The phone in my hand buzzed. Denise quickly took it and looked at a text.

"Is it them? Any word on Mackenzie? Is there a ransom?" I quickly asked.

A tight-lipped shake of the head. "It's just Gwen, my friend from work, asking how I'm doing."

"Is she aware of what's going on?"

"I called her on my way back to the apartment earlier, just before I ran into you. She's been a dear friend the last few months. She's my rock, helped me stay sober. I shared everything with her about what I found in the books at work. She even convinced me to reach out to you."

She typed something back to Gwen.

Hulama then started pinging Denise with questions about how this came to be. The questions were more detailed around the money-laundering process and what she'd found. It was obvious that Hulama understood the inner workings of accounting and how things should be set up. She nodded several times but showed no emotion.

After the Q&A session was done, Hulama tapped a finger to her chin. Her nails were painted a vibrant green.

"Is there anyone you can reach out to?" Keo asked Hulama. "Someone who might speak to you with strictest confidence?"

"Maybe," she said. "I can't poke the bear, though. There are many levels and branches of the Y-clan. In some respects, someone threatening to expose their ties to a supposedly legitimate business might set off an immediate and violent response. But honestly, they have so many people under their thumb…in the police, the press even. They've managed much worse situations and continued to do their business in their own way."

This crime syndicate seemed unstoppable, which in and of itself, was unsettling. But they had Mackenzie. My daughter. The fact that Hulama was wavering about how to approach this situation didn't give me a warm-and-fuzzy. Quite the opposite, in fact.

"There's got to be a way to get her back to us, safely. Money. An apology. Something, right?" I asked.

"You've heard nothing since she was taken?" Hulama asked Denise.

"Nothing."

"Go home," she said.

I traded a glance with Denise. "There's nothing we can do?"

"I will make a call and see where that takes me. Maybe, hopefully by morning, I can give you an update."

I looked at Keo, who said, "I don't want to get your hopes up, but there is the possibility that they're only trying to scare you. They could drop her off. You will want to be there. I will take you back to your car."

Denise headed for the door. I paused at Hulama's side. "Thank you. Who are you going to call?"

She glanced at Keo, then back at me. "You have a deep desire to know everything, but sometimes knowledge can bring you harm."

"It gives me hope. Are you going to share the name?"

"Kapule. I trust you will keep this connection to yourself."

Once in the minivan, we drove across the island as fast as the brakes would allow us.

Eight

The lone apartment complex in Fern Forest was a forgettable wasteland during the day. It was as though some type of apocalyptic event had pinpointed the dwelling while leaving nothing but breathtaking views across the rest of the Big Island. Under the cloak of darkness, however, the eerie factor skyrocketed.

Lights were not commonplace in many places across the island. In Fern Forest, they seemed to be a luxury that few could afford.

A rush of wind blew in from the wall of darkness, rattling screen doors. Empty paper cups and wrappers tumbled across the open area below as Denise and I made our way back to Unit E. Mackenzie was nowhere to be found. Denise checked everywhere in the apartment for any sign of a note, but everything was just as we'd left it.

I asked if she wanted me to make her something to eat.

"Not much in the place right now," she said, sitting on the couch, rubbing her face with both hands. "I haven't had a chance to make it to the store recently."

I searched the pantry and found a canister of pistachio mix. I walked into the living room area, held up the container.

"Mackenzie loves that as a snack." She swallowed hard, then sighed. "I'm not really hungry, though."

The unending emotional roller coaster was wearing her down. "If you want to keep up your strength, you might want to have some. We can buy more for Mackenzie when she gets back."

I was speaking about Mackenzie as if she were at a sleepover at a friend's house.

"Sure. I guess." I took a couple pistachios for myself and handed her the canister. My eyes were back on the print over her shoulder. The angle of the painting was looking down on the black-sand beach. Whitewater waves lapped against the shore.

"Where did you buy this painting?"

She chomped on some nuts. "Want to know the truth?" I was prone to offering up a sarcastic response, but now wasn't the time. "Hit me." I reached over and grabbed another handful of nuts and tossed them into my mouth.

"We did it together, me and Mackenzie."

I squinted my eyes and leaned closer. "Seriously?"

Denise chuckled. "I took up painting as I started my path to sobriety. Mackenzie would watch me all of the time, drawing pictures, coloring, sketching, doing something visual as I painted. A while back, we went hiking. I have this picture on my phone. One day, I started painting it, and she asked if she could help."

"She's only nine, and she can do this?"

"I did most of the ocean, but she painted the beach and most of the mountains."

In in the lower right-hand corner of the painting, I found their initials: DE + ME.

"Wow." My buddy back in Austin, an old high school friend named Tito, was an artist—and not the starving kind. He made good money painting nothing but Christmas vignettes. He'd found his true calling, he said. I knew he'd think this was incredible. I pulled out my phone and took a couple of pictures of the painting. "Where is this beach located?"

"Northwest side, on the North Kohala peninsula. It's the Polulu Valley Beach. We hiked down to the bottom. It's even more breathtaking if you're there."

"We'll go there…as soon as Mackenzie is back." I continued to find ways to act as if Mackenzie's return was imminent and very close at hand. I was trying to give Denise hope, but I was doing it just as much for myself.

Denise lifted from the couch. "I need to plug in my phone before I run out of battery." I followed her to the edge of her room. Behind her door, I found a wall of framed photos of her and Mackenzie, from when she was a baby on up to what appeared to be present day, including one where Mackenzie had a cape around her shoulders and was holding a wand, a playful but serious look on her face.

"What's going on here?" I pointed at the picture.

"It was Halloween from last year. She was Hermione."

The Harry Potter movies. Of course, any kid would be into that. I hadn't really thought about what a nine-year-old girl might be into.

"Where does she sleep?" I asked, looking around the sparse bedroom.

"Up until about a year ago, with me in the bed. But then she said she wanted to start being more independent. So she volunteered to take the couch. It folds out into a bed. I try trading with her on weekends when I'm not working, but she likes her own world. I think sometimes she gets up late at night and draws in her sketchpad."

Just then my eye caught a closed laptop on a tray. "The email you got that warned you about not going to the attorney general... Do you still have it?"

She nodded. "Want to see it?"

"Yep."

"My phone is so old, email isn't very reliable." She pulled open the laptop and logged in. A moment later, she was opening her email account. She pointed at the email with her finger and then clicked to open it up.

The message was exactly how she'd worded it. Not a surprise. My eyes went straight to the sender's email address: anonymous@bluegoose.com.

I forwarded the email to my personal account.

"What are you doing?" she asked.

"First, I wanted to make sure I have a copy." Then I opened a browser and searched for the bluegoose domain.

A million search results came back in under a second, or so the page claimed. I clicked on about thirty links through the first three pages, and none had anything to do with a domain of bluegoose.

"I'm not sure it's a real address," I said, rubbing my chin.

"That shouldn't be a surprise, right?"

"True," I said, still staring at the email, hoping somehow that a clue of Mackenzie's whereabouts would suddenly pop up on the screen.

She received another text from Gwen while we were staring at the laptop. I went into the kitchen, poured myself some water. She walked in a few minutes later.

"So I guess we wait until morning and hope to hear from Humala?" she asked, her eyes surveying the mess of dishes.

"I think it's best. We'll be here just in case…" I stopped short, but she knew what I meant.

"You can take the bedroom. I'll take the couch," Denise said.

"Says the girl who looks—"

"Hey, you know the rules. Never tell a girl she looks tired."

So true. I'd never had to use that phrase with Nicole. She had this youthful, vibrant look almost all the time. "I'm taking the couch," I said.

"Okay, okay. I'll throw you a pillow and blanket."

A few minutes later, she came out of her bedroom in a gown that stopped mid-thigh. She'd washed her face, put her hair up in a scrunchie. We made the couch into a bed, turned off the lights, and said goodnight. Ten minutes after she disappeared into her bedroom, I heard the floor creak. I could see her silhouette at the edge of my bed.

"You just going to stare at me? That's kind of creepy," I said.

"Do you mind?"

I pulled back the sheet. She put a leg on the bed, but stopped before snuggling up against me. "You're married, Ozzie. We shouldn't do this."

"This is nothing more than the parents of a little girl helping each other get through everything. Strictly platonic."

I felt like she'd smiled, but I couldn't be sure. She tucked in next to me.

We were still for a minute or so. Then she turned on her side and slowly rested her head on my chest. I could feel a small pull for Denise. But I knew most of it had to do with learning about Mackenzie, her kidnapping, and wanting to replace the anxiety with something positive.

"Your marriage... Is there something you're not telling me?" she asked out of nowhere.

"You read me pretty well."

More silence.

"I guess you don't want to tell me. That's okay."

"No, that's not it." I took in a deep breath. "Actually, I guess it is."

"I'm not trying to steal you from her."

"I know. Nicole and I had a great thing. Until it wasn't. Life is unpredictable. At least mine has been recently."

She squeezed my shoulder. "I'm sorry."

I kissed the top of her head. "Let's see if we can get some sleep."

A second later, the apartment door slammed open.

Nine

Denise shrieked directly into my ear, and my heart slammed into my chest. Heavy boots shook the floor as I swung back the sheet and tried to get out of the bed.

A soft glow from beyond the door outlined two men. Both appeared to have chrome domes. But I saw no smaller figure. No Mackenzie.

"Where is my daughter?" I demanded.

They didn't respond. The short one tripped over a kitchen chair, then tossed it against the wall like it was a pillow.

Denise was in my way. I pushed her off the bed until she landed on her butt. "Stay down!" I yelled, whipping around in a low stance.

I looked at the shadowy shapes of the intruders. "Tell us how we can get Mac—" I started.

The short guy plowed into my chest like I was a blocking dummy. And "dummy" was most fitting, because for some stupid reason, I'd thought they were going to listen to me, answer my question.

I tripped over a toy of some kind, slammed into the wall. A shelf of books and doodads rained on top of me, but that mattered very little. The tank of a man had crushed my lungs—I was unable to take in air.

A panic signal went off in my brain. The man was throwing punches into my gut. With everything I had left in me, I torqued right and sent the thug flying. He landed on a sharp corner of the fallen bookshelf. I could see him wincing in pain.

I got to my hands and knees and grunted out a breath. Relief.

"Ozzie, look out!"

I jerked my head to the side to see a boot headed for my rib cage. I quickly brought up my arm and twirled away. The boot— which was about as large as a water ski—slammed into my forearm. The pain was instant and intense. Was my arm broken? Maybe, but I saw an opening. Using my opposite hand, I grabbed the heel of his shoe and pulled up, springing to a standing position. His feet were swept off the floor, and he landed on his back and head.

"Where's my daughter, goddammit?" Denise yelled, suddenly at my side.

What was she doing? It was obvious they weren't here to negotiate or give us more information on turning over Mackenzie. "Get out of here," I screamed at her. "Run!"

The short one was back on his feet. I could make out his features a little better. He looked native to the island or somewhere in this part of the world and wore a Fu Manchu goatee. His arms looked like cannons. He lowered his stance, and I prepared for another hit.

Denise screamed something I didn't understand and ran toward the tank. She hurdled the other man, who was still trying to find his way to his feet.

"Stop!" I yelled instinctively. But a second later, she rammed into the tank, flailing her arms and feet. With one hand, he grabbed her wrist and whipped her behind him like she was a yo-yo. She hit the door to her bedroom and dropped to the floor.

The tank growled and ran right for me. I didn't budge for a couple of seconds. I wanted him to pick up speed and home in on an unmoving target. A blink before he reached me, I stuck out my leg, turning my body, and then hooked my arm under his and flipped him over my leg. He tumbled headfirst into a side table and lamp. I whipped my head around.

Denise wasn't on the floor. She was nowhere to be seen. Glancing out the apartment door, I saw no sign of her or any movement outside the door.

I quickly realized I should have never taken my eyes off the tall man. Something slammed into my head, and I stumbled backward until I hit the wall again. The blow had rocked me. Stars flashed all around as I fought to maintain my balance. It was a lost cause. I brought a hand to my head and felt a bump and a gash. The smell of copper filled my senses.

The tall man yelled and swung an arm at me. I caught a glimpse of a chain and a short, black baton—he had nunchucks. He let gravity take me to the floor. The weapon connected with my back, cracking me precisely on my shoulder blade. For a moment, my whole left arm tingled and then went numb. I writhed in pain, rolled over on the floor.

Another blink. I saw the dark ceiling, and, a second later, the tank leaped on me like a professional wrestler, his knees pounding into my gut. The compression was deep. My breath left me again, but I wondered if all my organs were still intact. I somehow found the energy to rock left and right, finally rolling him off me.

I looked up and saw the nunchucks a foot from my head. I realized my hand was on some type of notepad. I flipped it at the tall man's face. It threw him off a bit, and the nunchucks clipped my shoulder.

White-hot pain rippled down my arm, but I knew it was better than taking another blow to the head.

I had to get those damn nunchucks out of his hands. They were the great equalizer.

From the floor, I lunged for his knees—I might have hyperextended one or both of them. I grabbed hold of his lower legs. He pounded my back with an end of the nunchucks, but I didn't let go. I pulled back, but he wouldn't budge. I climbed to my feet just in time to get a baton to the face.

More stars. Now I tasted blood.

Before anther breath passed my lips, the tank grabbed me from behind, locking his arms behind my neck. The tall man came at me and whirled the nunchucks. I turned just in time for the baton to nail Tank in the head.

Bull's-eye. If I hadn't been in the fight of my life—where the hell was Denise?—I would have snickered.

I should have known better than to allow even a mental laugh. The tall man snatched his nunchucks and then flicked his wrist— the deadly baton was headed between my legs. I tried closing them, but I was too late. The nunchucks brushed my thigh, and then—as if it were programmed to find its target—connected with my groin. Actually, it thumped my right nut.

I folded like a cheap chair. On the way to the floor, a glint of light cut across his face, and I saw the guy sneering at me. His teeth didn't look human. Each one was jagged like a canine, but there were gaps in between each tooth. He had to be the ultimate case study for orthodontists.

A punch to the jaw from the tank, and I was down for the count. I looked up to see the tall man rearing back his arm for another bone-breaking crack with the nunchucks. I was cornered between the bed and wall. The tank was looming over me. No weapon in sight.

A crackle in the air, and sheet rock exploded above my head. Dust sprayed all over me and the tank. Someone had fired a gun.

Both thugs literally jumped in the air. Twisting and turning to escape, the tall man slipped and fell to the floor.

Denise was standing at her bedroom door, holding a gun with two hands.

"Where is my daughter?" she screamed to the point of shaking.

The tank lunged over me across the couch bed, then rolled off the other side. The tall man threw his nunchucks at her. They clanged off her shins. She dropped, but the gun went off again. Another misfire. This one hit the far wall just as the tank slipped out the apartment door. The tall man was right behind him.

I bear-crawled over to Denise, who was holding her shins, writhing in pain. I grabbed the gun from the floor and looked toward the door.

"Where is my baby, Oz? What have they done with Mackenzie?"

I didn't know the answer. "Are you okay?" I asked as blood trickled off my head onto her gown.

She didn't respond. She was too despondent.

I made it to my feet, tottered over to the threshold of the front door, and looked outside. Other than wrappers swirling in the wind, all was still. No sign of the men, a moving car, or even the glow of brake lights.

I looked at the gun in my hand, then turned back to Denise, who was limping toward me shaking her head, her hair matted to her wet face. Three feet from me, she broke down and pressed against my chest. My pain points were too many to count, but I knew it felt nothing like the agony in her heart.

Ten

I dug a fingernail into my forearm to try to divert the pain away from my face. My eyes shifted up to watch Denise's friend, Gwen, focus on the task at hand—using cotton balls to blot rubbing alcohol on my open cuts.

"I know this stuff is painful, but it will keep you from getting an infection. Trust me."

I clenched my jaw until she finished.

"Tough part is over, big man," she said, tossing the used cotton balls into the trash. Her little golden retriever, Sandy, ambled over and sniffed inside the open cabinet. "Always looking for a treat, aren't you, Sandy? Even at two in the morning," she said, rubbing his ears until he basically dropped to the floor in sheer ecstasy. She looked up at me with the start of a smile. "Just rub their ears, and it's pure heaven for a dog."

I started to lift my eyebrows, but that sent a stabbing pain into the open wound on my forehead.

She came back to where I sat at the kitchen table and examined my wound. "You're bleeding again, just from that little flicker of your forehead." More cotton balls, and then bacitracin and butterfly bandages.

I glanced over my shoulder and found Denise in the same position she was thirty minutes after Gwen had given her a clonazepam—conked out on the couch. Her hands were tucked under her face, which, surprisingly, was still hardened with stress.

"She needs her sleep," Gwen said, putting up the first-aid kit.

"Poor thing has been put through…" She paused.

"Hell?" I finished for her. Gwen made coffee and pulled two mugs from a cabinet that didn't shut all the way. The linoleum floor was stained and had punctures in it. The walls looked like they'd been painted during the Eisenhower administration. The house, nothing more than about eleven hundred square feet, tilted toward the back. This was barely a livable space, and it made me sad that she paid any amount to reside here.

"Sugar?" she asked.

"No thanks. Any flavored creamer?"

She looked at me as though I were speaking pig Latin.

"Black is fine, especially after tonight."

She sat on the other side of the wobbly table and sipped from her mug.

"You sure you two don't want to call the cops?"

"What?" I asked, sneaking another glance over my shoulder. "Oh, no. Denise would have my head. Keo said it was unwise as well."

A slow nod.

"I hope we're not putting you in danger. These guys mean business."

"I can see that. You're lucky to be alive."

I touched the bruise on my forehead. It was a doozy. "Seriously, if you're worried, I can put Denise in my minivan, and we can find a hotel to stay in."

"I'm not worried," she said, flicking her wrist. "You parked down the street."

She was either one fearless person or somehow had not understood what had taken place at Denise's apartment. "You and Denise are pretty close?"

She crossed her fingers. "Best friend I got on the whole island."

Her words showed loyalty, but her tone was flat, as if she were reading a script.

Give her a break, Oz. You've invaded her home in the middle of the night. Everyone deals with trauma in different ways.

I finally sipped from my mug. "How long have you lived on the Big Island?"

"About a year or so." She slurped down more coffee, as casual as any person could be. For a moment, I wondered if she'd taken one of those pills. Then again, she'd been quite handy with the first-aid kit.

"Do you work in the same department as Denise at Palm Tree Dreams?"

"I work in mergers and acquisitions, but I'm a bean counter like Denise."

"Have you been doing this long?"

"For a while. I used to be a school nurse back in the States, but something was missing from my life." She looked off into the distance. Her eyes seemed to be searching for an anchor. Finally, she settled her sights back on me.

I lifted my chin. "I'm sure you have some fun stories to tell."

She paused with her mug at her lips. "I think there's a lot of people who have old lives they wanted to leave behind on the mainland. It's good to put that part of my life behind me."

I wondered what event had compelled her to want to start a new life, especially on the island of Hawaii. The dog waddled up, and she reached down to pet him, her face expressionless and pale. She seemed void of emotion. Maybe it wasn't a life event as much as some type of tragedy that had scarred her. Hawaii was typically thought of as the ultimate escape. But it was rather obvious that crossing the Pacific Ocean didn't automatically seal you in a protective bubble. Denise was a good example of that.

Gwen's entire persona seemed to blend in with the drab walls. *Homely* was a word that came to mind. Long, flat hair that hung straight down, something akin to seaweed. The fact she wore no makeup wasn't surprising at this late hour, but I had the feeling she didn't own any. I saw no ear piercings. White, bland T-shirt with a faded logo of Penn State University. Gray, bland shorts. I looked around the kitchen again. No color of any kind. Even the one hand towel was an off-white shade.

To each her own, I supposed. At least Denise, if nothing else, still had energy and passion, even if a lot of it had been negative since we last saw each other in high school. Denise and Gwen seemed as different as two friends could be.

The dog scraped at the back door. "That's the sign," Gwen said, walking over to open the door and let him out. She watched him through the window. "Can't be too careful. All sorts of animals on the island could hurt Sandy, starting with snakes."

"That might be the worst kind of death," I said, making small talk.

She asked if I'd watch Sandy while she ran off to her bedroom. I lifted out of my chair, but paused before I took any steps. A pinch pulled at my stomach area—the kind that felt like a pair of pliers had just clamped down on a muscle or maybe some other internal organ. That countered the stabbing pain in about five other places. I made it to the back door, my eyes shifting from the dog, who was sniffing the grass and weeds like he was in hunting mode, over to Denise. I could see her chest lifting, and I wondered if her sleep was peaceful or if the torment of Mackenzie's abduction had stolen that part of her existence as well.

I took a few steps in her direction and saw blue-green bruises on her shins. I thought more about the assault. It seemed to have lasted forever, but looking back, the two men probably weren't in the apartment longer than sixty seconds.

They hadn't brought Mackenzie with them, nor had they even provided any feedback on where she was or how we could get her back. That had devastated Denise. Hell, it devastated me. Whether it was from witnessing her breakdown again, or just knowing it was my daughter—one I'd never seen or spoken to—who was being held by the people who nearly killed us, I could feel the emotional impact myself. I knew it wasn't the same as what Denise was feeling. It couldn't be. I just knew that the simple act of looking at Mackenzie's picture had made my heart bounce. My longing to get Mackenzie back and look her in the eyes was growing with each passing second, as was my concern for her well-being. She was a nine-year-old kid caught in a storm that no kid should have to face. She was *my* kid, though. And even as odd as that still sounded in my head, I couldn't hide my growing heartache.

My mind was pummeled with images of the tank and the tall man with the jagged teeth. One thing about their visit was abundantly clear: they were after me. With all the emotion of not receiving any information on how to get Mackenzie back, I wasn't sure if Denise had noticed that. Yes, they'd tossed her aside like a rag doll, and she'd suffered the bruises on her shins, but the focus of the beating was on me.

I just wasn't certain if they had intended on killing me—up until the moment that Denise fired her pistol—or if they were simply sending me some type of message to…

To do what, exactly?

How did Mackenzie's captors know I was on the island? Why would they care? We hadn't gone to the cops. Well, not the actual cops.

I reviewed everyone whom we'd told about Mackenzie and the *yakuza* holding her. Brook, my detective pal back in Austin. She'd shared it with Stan, the San Antonio detective. They were solid. And I doubted the *yakuza* had much of a presence inside those police departments. Regardless, I trusted Brook and Stan.

My thoughts went to Keo. The king of barterers. Was he trading favors with someone from the Y-clan, as he'd called it? He didn't seem like the type who'd harm a child, but it was obvious that he enjoyed the finer things in life. But what would he get out of having Mackenzie kidnapped? Hell, what was anyone getting out of holding Mackenzie? There had been no ransom demands.

What if they weren't holding Mackenzie? As much as my thoughts didn't want to go there, they could have already killed her. And maybe they would never formally convey that message. Maybe she'd been sold into slavery.

I could feel my throat tighten as I looked again at Denise. If either of those options had happened, she would shatter into a million pieces. And even though I'd yet to meet my daughter, I'd feel the pain too. The heart-wrenching pain.

Another angle pierced my thoughts. When we'd left the Green Dragon, Hulama was going to call her *yakuza* contact, a guy named Kapule. Had that call somehow triggered the violent response? They'd known we were headed back to the apartment.

Now every part of my body tightened, including my fists.

"Is something wrong?" Gwen appeared at the threshold to her bedroom door. Her eyes went to my fists.

I pushed out a breath and turned to see Sandy prancing around the back yard. "I'm fine. Sandy is just doing her thing."

"That assault still has you riled up, I guess."

I could feel my brow furrow, only because it tugged on my cuts. "Of course, it does. But I'm just…confused. Not sure which way to turn right now."

She walked past me and refilled her coffee mug, then asked if I wanted a second cup. I shook my head.

"So you're waiting to hear what this Hulama person comes back with?"

"Yep." I anchored my hands on the back of my chair, thinking about whether I should share my theory on how Hulama's call might have triggered the assault. Gwen was Denise's best friend, but I barely knew her. For now, I'd keep it to myself.

"You don't seem very optimistic." She walked to the door and let the dog back in. He scurried over to my leg and sniffed my shoe.

"I'm hopeful." I looked up, and she was staring right at me. "I have no other choice, really."

She nodded and moved on to reading the Bible. Yes, the Bible.

It appeared we all had our own ways of dealing with anxiety and the unpredictable future.

Eleven

The neighbor's roosters crowed the moment the sun peeked through the lush jungle to the east of Gwen's home. Ozzie and Denise had just taken off. She was standing in her back yard watching Sandy chase after a tennis ball, recalling the frantic state when the pair had arrived at her home about six hours earlier.

After giving Denise the clonazepam, she'd seized the opportunity to sit down and talk to Ozzie. To understand his motivations and what made him tick. It had been a fruitful discussion. A necessary one.

She pulled a cell phone from her shorts pocket and punched in the new number she'd been sent twenty-four hours earlier just for this purpose. It rang, but she could hear the sound hop, which was a sign that the call was being automatically redirected. It happened three times that she could detect.

The line was picked up.

"Joseph?" she asked.

A pause. "Please do not use my name. You should know the protocol by now."

"Oh, right. Sorry. I just got no sleep last night."

A few seconds of silence, then, "Do you have something to share?"

She tried to think of the correct phrase to use. "It's good news."

"It went as hoped, then?"

He suddenly had more energy to his voice, and this excited Gwen as much as the "good news."

"Yes, it did." Her voice cracked as emotion crept into the back of her throat. The separation of the last year would soon end. "When will I be able to come home?"

"All in due time."

"But you said I could—"

"Don't cross me." His tone was measured but direct.

She swallowed, reined in her emotions. "We're ready for the next phase, then, right?"

She thought she heard a huff, but it could have been the breeze in the air. He said, "I will commence phase two."

Relief. She'd reached her goal. And none too soon.

"We are very proud of the effort you have put in. You have paid your debt to your fellow tribe members."

"Thank you," she said as tears welled. "I can't wait to see everyone."

The line went dead. She stared at the phone a few extra seconds as Sandy barked at something over by the bushes. She called him inside and began to pack. Despite the uncomfortable phone call, she allowed joy to fill her heart. She was going home.

Twelve

I put down the one credit card I had that I felt reasonably certain wouldn't be rejected—a result of my odd non-living arrangement with Nicole—and pushed my half-eaten plate away from the edge.

The waitress, a gruff old woman who held a coffeepot in one hand, swung by and picked up the bill and the card. But she paused a second before moving on. She looked at me, then to the other side of the booth at Denise, who had her hands cupped over her mug. Denise was staring blankly through the murky glass windows into a parking lot full of motorcycles and beat-up cars.

"I think we're good on the coffee," I said, holding up a hand.

She nudged her head toward Denise and then tried to lower her volume. "She okay?"

It didn't work. I could see Denise's eyes flutter—yep, she'd heard the comment but apparently decided not to respond.

"She's fine. Just meditating some, I think."

The waitress shrugged, as if that line didn't really work for her, and walked off.

A yawn passed my lips before I could stop it. "You didn't eat much," I said.

"You either," Denise said, her sights still angled toward the parking lot.

I reached over and held my hand over her plate. "Do you mind?"

She tried to laugh but didn't quite get there. "You love your bacon."

"It's my weak spot, what can I say?" I ate the final piece in two bites, then wiped my greasy hands on a napkin.

"Any reply from Keo?" she asked.

The phone was on the table. I tapped the screen for the tenth time in the last ten minutes to verify what I already knew. "Nothing." I'd texted Keo just as we'd left Gwen's earlier, looking for an update on Hulama's call to her *yakuza* contact, Kapule.

"Do you think Hulama will be able to come through and—" Denise stopped short, bringing a hand to her face. More tears bubbled in her eyes. I reached across and put my hand on her arm.

"I know this isn't easy, Denise. It's tearing me up just watching you go through this."

She didn't respond for what seemed like a good minute but was probably no more than a few seconds. Then, without warning, she shoved her coffee away, sloshing it onto the table. She pointed a finger in my direction. She looked like she could chew through nails.

"Don't you care too, Ozzie? This isn't just my daughter. It's your daughter. Or, like every other guy out there, are you just going through the motions, waiting for your time to bail?"

Her words hung in the air like polluted smog. A couple of heads turned in our direction. I stayed silent.

The waitress came by and set the credit card and receipt on the table. As she searched her pockets, presumably for a pen, her eyes darted back and forth between me and Denise. She was smart enough not to make any comments. She walked off. I added the tip and signed it; then I began to slip out of the booth.

"Ozzie," Denise said, quickly reaching across the table to place her hand on top of mine.

I stopped and looked at her.

"I'm…" Her breath quaked. "I'm so sorry. I kept this secret from you for all these years, and when I finally reach out and ask you to come, you jump on the first plane. And now I treat you like shit."

"It's okay, Denise. I know this is crushing you. I just wish I could snap my fingers and make it all go away."

"I know you do. That's the kind of person you are." She cleared her throat. "Despite what I said, I know you care. You're doing everything you can to help bring Mackenzie home. You got beat up and almost killed, and yet here you are."

I nodded. "I'm not going anywhere, Denise. We can't undo the past. I just want to get Mackenzie back and see what life brings us."

She slid out of the booth and hugged me with everything she had.

Thirteen

As I gassed up the minivan, I spoke to Keo—for all of about five seconds. I asked if he'd heard anything from Hulama, and he said, "I'm on the phone with her right now. I'll call you back."

Denise and I waited anxiously in the minivan for the next twenty minutes. My phone sat in the cup holder, both of us staring holes in it.

"Is he just trying to fuck with our minds?" Denise asked.

"I think he's trying to help. He sounded sincere to me." I wasn't totally convinced of what I'd just conveyed, but I was still *hopeful*. The same term I'd used when describing my feelings to Gwen.

Five minutes passed. Another minivan rolled into the gas station's parking lot. The side door slid open, and three kids hopped out. The two girls, both probably just slightly younger than Mackenzie, were giggling as they raced inside. The boy, maybe an early teen, wore shades and had earbuds in his ears. He tried to pull off a swagger as he walked inside, as if he were too cool for his siblings.

"I've heard that boys are a pain in the ass to raise," Denise said.

"I'm sure we are." That drew a soft chuckle from Denise.

"Your dad. He was a real nice guy. Seemed like he was good with you and your brother, Tobin."

"Eh. I'm not sure his parental method would be used as the ultimate child-raising template, but yeah, somehow we got through those tough teenage years and learned a few things along the way."

The family exited the convenience store, each carrying a drink and a piece of fruit. Well, all except the cool one. He had to be different. He was chomping on a piece of beef jerky.

"Tell me I wasn't like that kid," I said.

"Are you kidding me? If you were, I would have never gone to prom with you."

We traded a glance and even found ourselves smiling. For the first time since she walked into her apartment two days earlier, I saw that sparkle in her eye. The same one I recalled from our teenage years, when life seemed far less complicated.

"We had some good times," I said.

"A lot of good times. Remember when your parents went on that weekend trip? Your brother was spending the night at a buddy's house, and you asked me to spend the night." She arched a playful eyebrow.

I scratched my chin. "Yeah, we pretended to play house, like we were real adults or something."

"We even slept in your parents' bed."

I nodded. "You're right—we did. Wow."

"But you're not remembering the funniest moment."

"By the look on your face, I think you mean funniest moment that happened to *me*."

She laughed. No, it was more like a cackle, and it warmed my heart. "You couldn't get my bra off."

"Really? But didn't we…you know."

"We did, only after I helped you out. I threw you a curve ball. I wore a bra that had the clasp in the front."

The memory finally came together, and I hooted out a laugh. "Well, besides, keeping my dad's lover a secret from my mom, that was probably my most stressful moment of high school."

I recalled having shared that part of my life with Denise way back when. She hadn't judged me or them; she was just there, always listening.

"I would say that was your most embarrassing moment, but you came through that weekend. Big time." She waggled her eyebrows.

I could feel my pale skin turn red. Nicole and I were still married but separated. We hadn't really established any rules before I'd jumped on the plane to Hawaii. It was just...complicated.

"Glad I could be of service," I said, which elicited another cackle from Denise.

All embarrassment aside, the levity was a nice break. It allowed me to think a little more clearly. I picked up the phone. "I want to give Keo some time. I don't want to spam-call the guy. But I think we need to come up with a long-term plan."

She nodded and rubbed her eyes. I suggested that I leave her at the gas station while I run to her apartment, pack a bag for her and grab my things, and then we could try to find a place to stay.

"Over my dead body," she said, twisting in her seat, as defiant as ever.

"Come on, Denise. It might be daylight outside, and I don't think the thugs are going to make a return visit, not this soon anyway, but I don't want to take any chances."

"But you will with your life?"

I turned my palms up and shrugged.

"I've thought more about their assault last night, Oz. They came to beat you up, not me. So, they view you as a threat."

"Maybe."

She tilted her head.

"Okay, so more than 'maybe.'" I glanced out the windshield and noticed how many bugs had been splattered.

"I'm going with you. What if we find something that has to do with Mackenzie? I want to be there. End of conversation."

I opened my mouth.

"Zip it," she said like a mom might say to her child.

"I was just going to ask if you want some beef jerky for the road."

One final laugh before heading back to the morbid apartment.

Fourteen

Puffy clouds rolled across the blue sky as we got out of the minivan at the apartment complex. I almost gasped when I saw kids actually playing near the dilapidated swing set. Two boys were throwing a Nerf football between the rusted metal bars.

As we walked up the steps, a man, maybe the dad, wearing his blue cap backward, came out to join them. Seeing the family unit outside made me feel more at ease. Perhaps this place wasn't a magnet for all things depressing and dangerous.

We walked up to Denise's apartment and found the door still locked. Good sign. Once inside, we both just stood there for a moment. The place was a wreck. We'd run out so quickly after the assault, we never took the time to assess the damage. Bookshelf was in pieces, books strewn everywhere. A side table was turned over; the aqua lamp had been shattered. After spotting the two bullet holes in the walls, my eyes found a sketchpad of drawings on the floor. A few of them were torn from the binder.

I leaned down and picked them up, along with the colored pencils. Based upon what Denise had shared, I could easily see Mackenzie's style in the drawings. Denise put her hand on my back, then walked into her bedroom to pack her bag. I placed the drawings in my bag and ensured I had all of my things together. A few seconds later, Denise rushed out of the bedroom.

"What's wrong?"

She pointed at the door. "I guess you didn't hear the knock."

My poor hearing strikes again. "Hold up," I said, but she had already begun to open the door.

A man was standing there. Something was in his hand. It was the guy in the blue cap, the one we'd seen earlier playing with the two kids.

"What is this?" she asked, staring at an envelope in his hand.

"It's for you," he said, extending his arm toward her.

"Do you know this guy?" I asked Denise.

"Seen him around." Then she looked pointedly at the man and said, "But I don't know your name."

"Look, I don't want to be a jerk, but I just picked up a hundred bucks to give you this envelope. So, here you go." The moment he handed it to Denise, I used two hands to grab him by the T-shirt. I twirled him around and smacked his back against the outside wall.

"Who gave this to you?"

His hat nearly fell off, but my grip was so tight he couldn't lift his arms. "Dude, I'm just the messenger."

"You said that already." I continued to apply pressure. "That's why I asked you who gave it to you."

"Just some teenage punk. He just walked up, gave me the hundred bucks, and told me to walk it up here. Then he took off. I swear, it's the truth. The cash is in my pocket, if you want to check."

I could feel my pulse hammering the side of my neck. I glanced at Denise, who was opening the letter.

The man continued. "I live right downstairs with my two boys. Do you think I'd be bullshitting you?"

I pulled back some.

"It's about Mackenzie," Denise said.

I let go of the guy, and he walked off. After shutting the door, she handed me the typed note. I read it out loud:

If you want to find Mackenzie, head east.

The mountains surge to the heavens, the coal runs deep, and the tribe became one. Where am I?

Please do not contact authorities or we will be forced to kill her.

Good luck.

We both tried to speak, but nothing came out. Denise's knees started to wobble a bit, and she gripped my shoulder. Finally, she said, "Ozzie, she's alive. But they've taken her somewhere. It sounds like she's..." She started to sway some as a new round of tears filled her red-rimmed eyes.

I nodded. "It sounds like they took her to the mainland." I was trying to fit this piece of the puzzle in with everything else we'd learned or experienced. But my mind couldn't make it work.

"Why...why would they take her off the island?" Denise began to sob. "I don't understand what they want. No ransom. No demands. They just take her, and now they send us this? I don't get it."

I took another glance at the note, then I pinched the bridge of my nose and tried to focus. "Coal runs deep. Coal runs deep."

"Has to be West Virginia, right?" she said, wiping away tears. She started shaking her head and ambled a few steps. "This just doesn't make sense, Ozzie. Why would the *yakuza* kidnap my daughter—"

"Our daughter," I quickly corrected her for some reason.

"*Our* daughter. I know the *yakuza* has a global presence, but *West Virginia?*"

She was in disbelief. I was right there with her. "I admit, it's hard to fathom." I walked past Denise, trampling across books and remnants of the broken lamp. Then, I flipped around and retraced my steps.

"Where are you going?"

"I don't know. Sometimes I just think better when I'm moving."

"Swimming?"

"Yeah, but that doesn't seem very realistic right now."

I continued pacing for the next minute, reading the letter every few seconds. I stopped on about my tenth lap. "Let's start with the basic facts and build from there, okay?"

"Okay, right." Her eyelashes fluttered as though they were butterfly wings.

"To state the obvious, this isn't one person. The term 'we' was used. That would make me think it was indeed the *yakuza* behind this. A well-organized team who would know how to get people…kids…off the island without unwanted attention."

She nodded. "I'm following you."

"But this note…it feels like they're teasing us. They want us to solve some riddle. Honestly, I'm just wondering what their point is. What's their end game?"

She spread her arms, then let them drop to her side. She didn't know the answer. I didn't know the answer. I was at a complete loss.

I flapped the paper in front of me. "This could all be a ruse. Someone could be getting off on watching us jump on a plane and run across the country. We can't dismiss that as a possibility."

"I know, I know." She clasped her hands and brought them to her forehead for a moment. "I just don't know what the fuck we should do."

A knock at the door.

We traded a quick glance; then I walked over and opened the door. "Keo?"

With his sunglasses covering his eyes, he wiped sweat from his forehead. "I thought you'd be here."

Fifteen

I picked chairs up from the floor and cleared off the kitchen table while Denise poured waters for all three of us. We sat down, explained to Keo what had transpired just minutes before he arrived, and handed him the note. He must have read it a dozen times, because his eyes—this was an assumption, of course, since I couldn't really see his eyes—never left the paper for a good five minutes.

"So, what do you make of this?" I asked.

He didn't lift his head. He just nodded.

"What?" Denise fired off. "What does that head-nod thing mean?"

He set the paper on the table. "In all my years on the force, I've never seen anything like this before."

"Do you think this is the work of the *yakuza*?" I asked.

He pressed his lips together and took in a deep breath.

"And?" Denise said sharply.

Another deep intake of air. "I don't know. My gut tells me *no*, but I've heard rumors that there are factions from the core group. Younger, more volatile. They think they are smarter than everyone, including their elders. This could be their work."

"*Could be*," I emphasized. "How do we know, dammit?" I bit the side of my cheek, which kept me from slamming a fist on the table…or through the table.

Denise picked up her glass of water and chugged it; then she wiped her mouth on her arm, her eyes never leaving Keo.

"Hold on a second," he said, scooting up in his chair. "My update from Hulama. She and I were talking when you called me earlier."

"Right," I said. "What did she learn?"

"Kapule denied having any knowledge of the kidnapping."

Denise and I locked eyes for a quick second.

"So, that's good news, I guess? I don't even know at this point." Denise dropped her elbows to the table.

"But," Keo said, holding up a finger, "he did tell Hulama that he couldn't rule out some type of rogue group that might have gone off and done something like this."

"Okay, wonderful. More vague responses. It's like dealing with a politician."

"I believe Kapule's position in the *yakuza* is quite political, as a matter of fact."

I twisted out of the chair and walked across the living room, tripping over a part of the bookshelf before turning back around.

"I sense your frustration, Ozzie. And Denise, I know this is gut-wrenching," Keo said, placing his hand to his chest. "For everything you have experienced here on the Big Island, please know how sorry I am. This does not represent what my people are about."

"Thanks, Keo," I said, raking my fingers through my hair. "This isn't an indictment on the Hawaiian people, or even the Japanese. This island is beautiful in so many ways…to the point of making you speechless. But no place is immune to the twisted and—"

"Fucked-up people!" Denise said, smacking her hand off the table. "We still don't know who took my Mackenzie. Maybe it's the *yakuza*, maybe it's some type of splinter group. Who knows?" She paused a second, her eyes landing on the painting over the couch. "And beyond that, we're not sure if we should try to solve this riddle and chase after something that might be a complete fucking farce!"

I walked back over to the table and rested my hand on Denise's shoulder. I could feel the tightness in her muscles and ligaments.

There was a moment of silence, and then Keo spoke up. "Just so you know, Kapule said he does not condone this type of retribution. And that he will continue seeking more information. If he learns of anything, he will relay it to Hulama."

Trusting a *yakuza* insider to provide the key piece of information that would lead us to Mackenzie seemed like an unwise choice. Not that I'd turn anything away at this point.

I picked up the note and read the riddle once again.

The mountains surge to the heavens, the coal runs deep, and the tribe became one. Where am I?

I looked at Denise. "I think at least one of us needs to follow this riddle. And I think it needs to be me."

She clenched her jaw but didn't immediately respond.

"Well?" I asked.

"I want to come with you. I need to come with you."

"Do you think that's wise? I mean, part of me thinks that whoever has her—the *yakuza*, a splinter group, or some other group—is trying to test our resolve. That could mean us finding this location, or it could mean we sit here and call their bluff. We hurt our chances by having two people in the same place, right?"

· "Maybe," she said, looking down.

"I will stay here. Live here at your apartment," Keo said.

Denise and I both looked at Keo. I said, "Are you sure? I mean, this isn't exactly the Four Seasons resort. And this is two hours away from the other side of the island."

"But this is your daughter," he said. "It's too important. I will stay here. I will let you know if any information is dropped off."

I looked to Denise, then back to Keo. "Thank you."

"This means a lot, Keo. I can't tell you how much your help means to me," Denise said, wiping a tear off her cheek.

We packed up and made our way to the door. Keo was washing dishes in the kitchen, already in cleanup mode.

"I'm sorry this place is such a wreck," Denise said.

"No worries. I just have to keep my mind busy. It's either clean or play online golf. I think I'd rather clean."

"Hey," I said. "Be careful. This could be dangerous for you."

"No worries. I drove my ghetto car over here, and I have a .357 magnum in it. I'll bring it inside and just dare anyone to screw with me." He smiled, his teeth almost glimmering.

Denise gave him a hug, and I shook his hand.

As we headed out the door, Keo tapped my shoulder. I did the same to Denise, and we turned around to face him. Keo said, "There is an old Hawaiian proverb that you need to know. A'OHE PU'U KI'EKI'E KE HO'A'O 'IA E PI'I."

I shrugged.

"It means," he said, "no cliff is so tall it cannot be climbed."

I let those powerful words energize me on the way to the airport.

Sixteen

The even cadence of the drumbeats outside of his hut could be felt in his chest. He slowly closed his eyes, allowing his mind to find the tranquility required for such an affair. His power to immerse himself in the moment had surprised even himself. He'd once found himself able to match the pace of his heart with the thud of each drumbeat. Who would have thought that the country boy with no advanced education and diagnosed with ADHD could exercise such self-control?

Control indeed.

He slipped on the robe he'd worn dozens of times for this meaningful ritual and walked to the threshold of the door. It opened, and he saw the men and women of the tribe part like the Red Sea, giving him a clear path to the pit that crackled and popped with flames at least five feet high.

The drums beat louder now, and he could feel the energy in the space from the mass of people, as well as the spiritual presence of...Him. That familiar surge was like oxygen. Actually, it was more like the ultimate injection of power. One that bolstered his self-image—that he could not deny. But he knew the responsibility that lay at his feet. It was something that he neither shied away from nor reduced in importance for those who lived within their confines, or even those in the outer world. In due time, everyone who walked the planet would see this ultimate result of their plans. His plan.

Cecelia appeared to his right, a solemn look on her face. She nodded once to signal everything was in place. He moved one step forward. She leaned in, whispered in his ear. "The fervor is growing. They are excited but also anxious for the new arrival."

His eyes remained focused on the scene at the front of their ritual space.

She added, "Joseph, you must promise them it will happen soon. We cannot lose this opportunity."

"Thy will be done," he said.

She stepped aside, allowing Joseph the full command of the group. He methodically made his way down the dirt path. He felt not only the warmth of the fire up ahead but also the many pairs of eyes on him.

The closer he got to the front, the more the roaring fire drowned out the beat of the drums. The canopy of trees made the dark night even darker, which only presented the flames in a more dramatic fashion. It was one of the reasons this location had been selected. But certainly not the most important.

He approached the altar set up next to the fire pit and eyed the creature that had already been killed. He picked up the cup of blood from the sacrifice; then he turned and faced the tribe.

"My friends, we have come together again to celebrate our lives together, to honor those who have made the ultimate sacrifice, and those who will do so in the future."

He paused to admire the head nods and warm smiles. He then raised the cup. "As it states in Isaiah, 'He was oppressed and He was afflicted. Yet He did not open His mouth. Like a lamb that is led to slaughter, and like a sheep that is silent before its shearers. So He did not open His mouth.'"

He then drank from the cup of blood. The crowd clapped, and a few even shouted out in praise. He was fine with this outpouring of affection. In fact, he knew it was infectious for the other men and women to hear this level of support, especially those on the fringe of their movement.

He set the cup on the altar and grabbed the end of a metal rod, shifting it until the opposite end was over the fire. There were no squeals or desperate pleas—those had been contained to three members of the tribe who'd refused to follow the agreed-upon commandments of the tribe.

This time, like almost all of the others, they sacrificed a lamb—just as the Bible had stated. He turned and faced his brethren.

"And we will finish with our typical scripture reading from Exodus. Everyone join with me now."

The group then said in unison, "You shall take the ram of ordination and boil its flesh in a holy place."

He smiled as he brought his hands together and lifted them to the sky. "Your patience on our mission will be rewarded," he said as the beat of the drums again grew louder. "The one I've promised, the one who will bring us deliverance, will be unveiled at a time very close in the future. And that is when we will see the return of His essence into our tribe."

The group clapped and cheered as he exited the ritual space and made his way back into the hut. Cecelia walked in as he was hanging up his robe. He waited for her response.

"Another masterful performance. This might buy us a little bit of time. But we cannot fail them. If we do, then that could be the end of Kingdom."

Seventeen

The moment Denise and I arrived at the Kona International Airport in Hawaii, we had all of about ten minutes to decide if we wanted to take the very next flight into Los Angeles or do more research and consider finding another flight directly into an airport farther east.

Our initial research into one part of the riddle had countered what I'd believed for most of my life: that West Virginia was the state that produced the most coal. Remarkably, that honor went to Wyoming. With that uncertainty looming over our decision, we went with the safe bet and took the flight to LAX. We tried doing some work on the flight, but between the constant orders to put up our devices, or move out of the way of the guy at the end of our row so he could use the restroom or pass him food or another drink refill, it was basically wasted time.

Well, not exactly. Both of us got in some needed shut-eye. When I awoke, Denise was drooling on my shoulder, and she had one hand on my crotch. I was sure the two events were completely unrelated.

Once we landed, we camped out in TGI Fridays, ordered an assortment of appetizers and a carafe of water, and went to work.

I brought my phone to eye level. "I've pulled up the list of flights leaving LAX into the continental US for the next twelve hours," I said, taking a bite of celery.

"So that's how you keep the washboard abs?" Denise said, pulling apart a stick of fried cheese. "Eating like a bird?"

"Birds don't eat celery. It will kill them. If I don't eat something remotely healthy, I get grumpy."

"Oh, so the great Oz does have a flaw." She raised an eyebrow — one that wasn't all that playful.

"Funny." I would have hit her with a sharp comeback, but now wasn't the time. I was just happy she'd picked up a couple more hours of sleep. The tug on her emotions had been taking its toll. Somehow, she looked even thinner than when I first saw her. Hopefully the feast of fried foods could add a little meat to her bony frame.

"I'm ready to go." She wiped her hands on her napkin, then opened the browser on her phone.

I pulled out the note, and she eyed the piece of paper like it might reach out and slit her throat. "It's okay. I just think we'll want to reference the riddle a few times as we narrow down our options."

A shadow crossed her face, and the hint of perkiness was wiped away. I tried to keep the energy positive and focused on the facts.

"The riddle has three basic pieces. The mountains surge to the heavens, the coal runs deep, and the tribe became one."

"No clue what the hell is meant by that 'tribe' shit," she said, picking up a piece of celery, then dropping it back on the platter without taking a bite.

"That's the toughest one. Let's get back to the coal question first."

"I have the site pulled up right here. Top ten coal-mining states in the country. I already told you Wyoming was number one, but do you know by how much?"

"Hit me." I sipped my water; then I realized how dehydrated I was and chugged until the ice clanged the side of the cup.

"Almost four times more coal is produced in Wyoming than in West Virginia, the number-two state on the list."

I strummed my fingers on the table. "I wonder which of those states on your list have mountains."

"Kentucky?"

"You don't sound so certain."

"I'm not sure if the state has mountains. I'm not great with geography. Numbers, yes; geography, not so much. I know they have horses. I dated a guy for a while whose family owned a horse-breeding farm."

In a normal setting, I could see us sharing a lot of our past lives, but right now any new information was nothing more than cute anecdotes. "I know the Appalachians run through Kentucky. Probably not the tallest mountains, but lots of trees. Very pretty, from what I recall."

"You've been there?"

"Took a road trip through the east with some friends when I went to law school at Georgetown."

She nodded.

Another anecdote that we'd have to ignore for now. Maybe later, once we had Mackenzie back, we could all share stories. I hooked my hope onto that thought.

"Any other states on your coal-mining list that have mountains?"

"Pennsylvania is number four, Illinois number five, Montana at number six, and Texas at number seven."

"Okay, stop right there. We both know that outside of the Hill Country, Texas is as flat as this table."

"Good point." She held up a finger, then tapped her screen about a dozen times in four seconds. Then she reached over and grabbed another cheese stick. It was obvious she was waiting for a browser window to open.

"Okay," she said, chomping on the last of her cheese stick. "The highest mountain in Wyoming is Gannett Peak. Almost fourteen thousand feet high. Fremont Peak is only two hundred feet shorter. On and on the list goes."

She tapped the screen again, then took a quick drink. "Okay, on to West Virginia. Their highest peak is forty-six hundred feet."

"The Allegheny and Shenandoah mountain ranges," I said.

"Your law-school trip?"

I nodded.

"I'm not impressed," she said, arching an eyebrow.

"Don't worry. Most girls aren't." Before she could laugh, I said, "Moving on."

"All right, Kentucky is nipping at the heels of West Virginia, about five hundred feet behind. Black Mountain—that sounds ominous—comes in at just over forty-one hundred feet."

"What about Pennsylvania? Probably not much there, right?"

"Eh. More than Texas. Highest peak is thirty-two hundred."

"Refills on your water?"

We both turned to the waiter. He could have been me ten years ago. "Sure, thanks."

He did his thing and gave us back our personal time.

"If we stick with the facts, Wyoming is number one in both categories," Denise said. "You want to start looking for flights into— Wait. What's the largest city in Wyoming?"

"Cheyenne," I said, scanning the list of flights on my phone. "Earliest flight is tonight, about ten hours from now. But I don't think we should book the flight until we figure out the answer to number three." I let that sit there for a moment, then, "Let me amend that statement."

She gave me a mock salute. "Sure thing, Counselor. You may proceed."

I smirked. "Anyway, we can't look at these as three separate and equal pieces. The piece we have no real clue how to tackle— the cryptic notion about a tribe becoming one—could be the only thing that matters to these people."

She let her arm drop to the table. "What do we expect to find when we get to this place…if we can ever find it?"

"While you were sleeping on the plane, I was wondering the same thing."

"I mean, is Mackenzie just going to be standing at the top of a mountain with a note attached to her saying, 'Here you go'? Or are we going to find a camp setup, or even a town?" She curled her lips inward. She was stressed because she couldn't envision how this would work. I couldn't either.

"One step at a time, Denise. We'll figure it out, though. Okay?"

She nodded.

"So, we know the leading candidates for tall mountains and coal production." I looked at the note again. "*Tribe became one.* I wonder if this is where we have to get more specific. City, town, community…"

"Or peak?"

"Maybe."

"Should I look up Native American tribes and their locations?" she asked.

"Sounds too literal, but the process of elimination might be the most prudent way to make progress."

She typed in her search keywords.

A moment later, "Holy shit."

"What?"

"Did you know there are five hundred sixty-two tribes, bands, nations, pueblos, rancherias, communities, and Native villages in the US?"

"What's a rancheria?"

"Fuck if I know." She puffed out a breath. "Good news, though. Almost half—two hundred twenty-nine—are located in Alaska."

"And the bad news?" I asked.

"The remaining ones are spread through thirty-three other states."

"Ouch." I took another bite of celery and went back to the note. The key to a riddle was trying to understand the meaning behind all of the words. But how obvious or obscure was the answer? Was it at a second-grade level or doctorate level?

"Why are you shaking your head?" she asked.

"Didn't know I was." My eyes were diverted by the man behind Denise, who had picked up his newspaper and was trying to fold it back to its original form. He looked like he was wrestling an amoeba.

"What are you staring at?"

"Doesn't matter. I think we need to start searching for tribes or words that say something about *When the tribe became one.* That's an event. It could have been in the news."

Denise put in the search terms and waited. "Okay, when I enter 'tribes,' all I get is generic information like I'd shared earlier. How many there are, where they're located, blah, blah blah." She kept her eyes focused on the screen and did a second search. "I changed the search to 'tribe news,' and…" She dropped the phone to the table, sat back, and crossed her arms, her face painted with frustration.

"What?"

She nodded toward the phone. I turned it around, looked at the screen, and found a number of stories on the Cleveland Indians baseball team. I tapped over to the second page of results. "There seems to be more stories about actual tribe news—not baseball related—here on page two and going forward. We could click on each of these stories."

"Did you see how many results came back? Over twenty million. We don't have time to validate twenty million links. Even if it's twenty thousand or two thousand, that will take us hours and hours. We're not getting any closer. Fuck!"

We needed to adjust our strategy. I had to figure out how.

Eighteen

While Denise went off to the ladies' room, I stayed in my seat and immersed myself in the riddle. I must have read it another twenty times, pausing on each piece of the riddle, then studying how specific words from the three components of the riddle might be related.

I rubbed a hand across my face as I sat back and looked around. Droves of travelers hustled past the open café. Kids trying to keep up with their parents. Some pouting; others actively crying. I saw one toddler in his dad's arms, smacking his dad in the face.

Parenthood. Was I ready for it? Mackenzie was well beyond the terrible twos. She was nine. I wondered how close to ten she was. Was that a big deal, having that first double-digit birthday? I knew my whole mindset would have to change. Once I found her. But what would she say to me? I'd never asked Denise if she'd told Mackenzie about me. Surely, she would have wondered who her dad was…where he was. Maybe Denise made up a story of some deadbeat dad. I would ask, but only when the time was right. Which wasn't now.

My sights went back to the man reading his newspaper, *USA Today*. He looked like a business traveler. A closed laptop was on the table. He was wearing reading glasses that were a little off-kilter. Probably because of his nose, which was crooked. I had a friend in high school who'd broken his nose when he dove for a football and rammed his nose into his brother's head.

That could have been me and Tobin. We clowned around a lot as kids. Now he was off conquering the startup world. Part of me couldn't wait to get back to Austin, to show off my new daughter to everyone. But there were as many questions back there as there were outside of my home bubble, starting with Nicole. She was living in our home. She'd had an affair for the last two or three months. Hell, we'd only been married six months. She had been the center of my world, the love of my life. Or so I'd thought. But I could see that changing with Mackenzie entering my life. Any other thoughts of Nicole and where we stood would have to wait.

Then something leaped to the front of my mind: *Who says Mackenzie would live in Austin?* Denise might want to stay in Hawaii. The thought of that looming discussion twisted my stomach into a major-league knot.

A headline from the man's newspaper snagged my gaze: "Televangelist Files for Bankruptcy: Says Followers Will Bail Him Out."

I looked back at the riddle. *Where the mountains surge to the heavens.* If taken literally, *heavens* could be a religious reference.

Heavens.

Denise arrived at the table, and I shared my latest thoughts.

"Damn, that's why your parents paid big bucks for you to go to law school."

For whatever reason, her comment triggered a question about my real parents. Too much to deal with for now, so I pushed the thought aside and watched Denise go to work with various searches.

"Have anything yet?" I strummed my fingers on the table, twice as fast as last time.

"Now who's the impatient one?" she said, her eyes never leaving her phone.

She started mumbling as she reviewed search results, but I wasn't paying much attention. I was too focused on my latest idea—"heavens" and what that could mean.

Then I shifted my eyes to the last piece of the riddle. *"Where the tribe became one,"* I said out loud. Tribe. Wait. That was a term found in the Jewish religion. I was Jewish. Well, I hadn't been to temple in years. My parents had Jewish roots going back to Poland. They were never embarrassed by those roots, and they really played them up in certain social circles. While growing up, it seemed like a bit of a farce, but I went with it. Just like everything else with my adoptive family.

I blinked and retrained my thoughts on the two words I believed might be connected. "Hey," I said, tapping my hand on the table.

"Hay is for horses." With her eyes still glued to her phone screen, Denise started to smirk but never quite got there. "Can't you see I'm busy?"

"Let's change the search terms. Try 'heavens' and 'tribe' together. We need to focus on potential ties to religion."

She glanced up. "Religion."

"You a nonbeliever?"

"In God or you?" Now she smiled.

"Good one." I explained the connection of "tribe" to Judaism.

She nodded while munching on a nacho. "I would have never made that association. But I like the thought. Give me a second."

A second turned into a minute.

"And?"

"And you're impatient."

I leaned forward and set my elbows on the table.

"I can feel your breath on me."

"Is that a bad thing?" I realized how flirtatious that sounded the moment the words left my mouth. I didn't feel that way about Denise. It was more the bond I felt from learning that we shared a child.

"That guy next to me on the plane had breath that could have bored a hole through steel. So, comparatively, your breath is like a fresh mint."

"Thanks." I drank from my cup of water and leaned back.

She told me that the top search results for "heavens" and "tribe" were related to Beast Tribe Quest, some type of online game.

"Are you serious?" I asked. I rubbed my face again.

"Like a heart attack."

I paused for a second. I hadn't told her about my dad and his death from a heart attack, even if one of his long-time associates had killed him. Of course, she'd claimed his heart was about to stop anyway. I got past it. "The gaming community. There are some real nutjobs in that world."

"And more importantly, could they really be with the *yakuza*?" she asked, a hand to her chin.

I opened my mouth, but she spoke first.

"That was a rhetorical question. I know Keo and that Kapule guy said there could be splinter groups, even suggesting that younger members of the crime organization could be involved."

"*Yakuza* and online gamers are like this, don't you know?" I joked, crossing my fingers. "Honestly, at this point, I have no idea. And to think this all started because you found evidence of money laundering. It's hard to fathom."

Her shoulders dropped. "Are you thinking the *yakuza* may not be involved?"

I shrugged. "Maybe Hulama's contact, Kapule, was telling the truth when he said he couldn't find any evidence that his group was behind this. I know it sounds strange when 'truth' and a *yakuza* member are mentioned in the same sentence."

She pushed a lock of hair out of her face, her eyes searching for a place to land. She was questioning this whole process. So was I.

"Look, we're sitting in LA, and we've got a note in front of us that could be the key to getting Mackenzie back."

"You said *could.*"

She was looking for absolutes. In this twisted nightmare, I didn't see a single one. But I couldn't give her the glass-half-empty perspective. She needed hope.

"I don't know what these people are thinking, or their motivation. They haven't asked for money. If they had other plans for Mackenzie—the types of things we really don't want to think about—then I can't see them reaching out and giving us this note."

I picked up the piece of paper, glancing at the words for about the thousandth time. "They said they don't want to kill her. They even said 'good luck.' It's like they want us to find this location…to find her. Why take her and play this game, I have no clue. As tough as this has been on you—and I might need a new lining to my stomach when all of this is over—this could get tougher. We have to dig deep and find a resolve that allows us to deal with the peaks and valleys, to keep our sanity. For Mackenzie."

Tears welled in her eyes, but she somehow kept the flow in check. "For Mackenzie."

We both took sips from our water glasses, then refocused our efforts on figuring out the answer to the riddle. Both of us started plugging in any type of search terms that related to heaven, tribes, religion—in a general sense and individual ones.

Denise put her hand out.

"Oh, did you say something?" I asked.

"Did you know there are an estimated one thousand religious cults in the United States? They say the exact number is unknown because some do not like to advertise their existence."

"Okay. Let's add 'religious cult' to our search terms."

"Got it. Wouldn't it help, though, if we split up the search terms? Save us a little time, right?"

"Normally, I'd agree, but it would take us just as much time to document everything and then split it up. I say we just both search for everything that comes to mind. If we feel like we're getting warm, speak up, and then we'll pivot to focus on a smaller subset of terms."

She ate the last bite of a nacho and started tapping her screen with renewed energy. Damn, I was proud of her. Most parents—and I exclude myself from this group, since I didn't really qualify—would wilt under this type of pressure. Her daughter had been kidnapped, possibly by a global crime syndicate, maybe by some other group. She'd been told her daughter would die if she went to the authorities. And now we were chasing down the answer to a riddle—a frickin' riddle—hoping Mackenzie would be alive and well once we got to this secret location. It sounded like we were acting out a scene from *Batman*, starring the Riddler.

"Hmm," she said just as I stretched my fingers until my knuckles popped.

"Hmm what?"

She bit her lower lip, then twisted her head while staring at the phone.

"Who's hard of hearing now?" I asked. I was okay with a little self-deprecating humor.

"I'm reading this story from a year ago or so. Talks about this religious cult in the mountains of West Virginia." She lifted her head. "They called it Camp Israel."

A zap of electricity connected with the base of my skull. Without saying a word, I leaned over the table and read the full story over her shoulder. We researched the topic for another thirty minutes. Along the way, we also found references to other cults, including an active one in Wyoming, outside of Cheyenne. Something called the Scripture Society. We then put in more time trying to learn about that group. They were rumored to be holding people against their will, and there had been reports of rape and incest. They had also built up a large cache of weapons, according to one report, so authorities were hesitant to raid the place.

It was down to two places.

Nineteen

We spent the next thirty minutes debating the merits of both locations, which, as I pointed out, also meant we were debating the merits of two religious cults.

On the surface, the Wyoming location should win hands down. Tallest mountains—check. Most coal production—check. They also had some type of so-called "tribe"…which, keeping with our premise, we'd interpreted as a group of folks bound by a religious affiliation, those who had shared goals and values. The Scripture Society fit that bill.

"More than anything, Oz, they're active," Denise said of the Scripture Society. "They have some type of agenda—all these cults typically do. We just don't know what it is, exactly. I think that gives them the advantage. We don't know if that Camp Israel has anyone around. The story said the leaders had been arrested after fleeing the country. I think they're actually serving time in a federal prison."

This caused me to pause. I stared at the man with the wrinkled newspaper and rethought my logic. Then, I laid my palms on the table, which I immediately regretted—my hands were quickly coated with invisible sticky goo.

She handed me a wet napkin, and I wiped off my hands. I said, "You're right on all of those points. And if this had happened anywhere in the contiguous states, I might agree with Wyoming. But this all started in Hawaii. That's not someplace you can just drive to. Most people wouldn't think about going over there unless they were on vacation or something really important drew them there. I keep going back to what spurred this kidnapping—your discovery of money laundering. The *yakuza* were the only ones who could feel threatened by you spreading news of that crime. I know this Kapule fellow has denied his group is connected to taking Mackenzie, but there still remains a possibility that some part of that group could be involved."

I gave myself a moment to replay what I'd just said, to see if I believed it. And also to see if Denise would revolt. Following a thirty-second span in which she studied her phone and then looked at me while twirling a lock of hair around her finger—all in silence—I made my final argument.

"The Wyoming group is on lockdown mode, by the sound of it. They might have some twisted agenda that we're not aware of, but why would they kidnap a girl, bring her to their facility? That would only invite more heat, not less. On the other hand, this location in the mountains of West Virginia... Where did you say it was, exactly?"

"Uh..." She checked her phone. "In a rural area near a small town called Parsons."

"It's in the middle of nowhere, and I'm guessing that it's either abandoned or maybe even been destroyed. Let's just say I doubt they've built high-rise condos on the property. So, what better place for a group like the *yakuza*, or some offshoot of that group, to set up a small camp? It might just be four or five people involved here."

She started nodding. "How confident are you?"

I put a finger to my chin. "Maybe a whopping fifty-two percent. But, in an election, that means I'd have the mandate of the people," I said with an authoritarian tone.

"Now you sound like the make-believe voice of the wizard from Oz."

Everyone had to make a joke about my name. I understood it was too easy to pass up. "Haven't heard that one before," I said with an obvious eye roll.

"So, you're on board with the West Virginia location?"

She waggled her phone between two fingers and let a smile slip through her lips. "I have a map pulled up. Need to fly into DC. Reagan or Dulles?"

I booked us on the earliest flight available, which would put us into DC at almost 10 p.m.

Twenty

The moment the plane landed at Dulles Airport in our nation's capital, I turned on my phone to validate directions toward what had been called Camp Israel. While the location appeared to be due west from DC, the rural highway system would wind us through the Shenandoah Mountains. I knew Virginia rather well. I'd visited Charlottesville a few times—I had a buddy who went to the University of Virginia. But I'd only been in West Virginia a single time, and that was more of a blur. I mostly remembered seeing beautiful, rolling mountains cast in shades of rust—it was fall at the time—countered with pockets of communities that looked as though they'd been plowed over by military tanks. It was a depressing scene, from what I could recall.

The cross-country flight took its toll on our energy levels. Denise didn't say much as we inched forward while exiting the plane. I felt my phone buzz twice in about twenty seconds. I pulled it from my pocket and checked the screen. Two text messages. One from Steve Gartner, the other from Nicole. I clicked on the easy one first—Steve's.

Dude dropped by saying he hadn't heard from Ray in a week. Wanted update on his case. Ray said you were the man now. Is that true?

I wondered if this might happen. Ray had been the long-time PI used by Novak and Novak. I'd used him a few times. He'd done a lot more work for my dad. When I'd asked Ray to help find the mystery person who had killed my dad, it had triggered a violent response. Two members of a gang, MS-13, had come to Ray's office and beat the crap out of him. When I showed up at his office, he was sprawled out on the floor, bleeding profusely, almost unrecognizable. After spending a few minutes to tend to his wounds, Ray unlocked a filing cabinet and pulled out what he affectionately called his "Shit Hit The Fan" bag. It had cash, essential clothing. Might have been a new identification in there somewhere. Regardless, he hit the road, saying if he didn't leave then, he'd be a dead man. And he strongly suggested I do the same.

When I said I wasn't going to run from the thugs or the man who'd hired them, and knowing my old firm was being sold off and I didn't have much desire to continue in the legal field, he came up with an idea. He said I should take over Ray Gartner Investigations and that he'd drop his brother a quick line and fill him in—which made sense because his PI office was in the back of Steve's automotive shop—and then take off. He'd said no one would be able to find him.

Just like that, Ray was off the grid. Not two days later, I received the note from Denise saying I was a father and Mackenzie was in danger.

To say my life had been a whirlwind in the last ten-plus days would be like saying the Pacific Ocean was a puddle of water. But I wasn't blind. I knew life would return to normal, eventually. What that looked like at this point was hard to imagine. Still, though, I yearned for heading back to Austin with Mackenzie and Denise, setting up some type of co-parenting arrangement. Which also meant I needed cash flow. *Why not give the PI thing a whirl?*

With the cattle-crawl out of the plane at another standstill, I typed a quick response to Steve.

Dealing with a little personal situation. Hope to have it wrapped up in a few days. Tell the client and anyone else looking for Ray that his silent partner will be back shortly and take care of everything.

The procession moved another six or seven feet until two men clogged the aisle because they were arguing over who should go first in the line. Seriously, preschoolers would have been better behaved.

"Dear God, tell me this isn't happening," Denise said, leaning back to whisper into my ear. "Guys always have to show off who has the biggest pair. In my book, both of these fools are—" Her voice had risen as she neared the end of her statement.

I rested my hand on her shoulder before she said it. The last thing we needed was an all-out brawl. I smiled at her; then my phone buzzed again. Steve had responded.

Can't believe you'd take over that shithole office, but I won't touch a thing. Let's talk when you're back in town.

Ray's office would have been a great hiding spot for kids playing hide-and-go-seek. Stacks of newspapers, magazines, and other . . . crap were piled six feet high. Ray had needed to frickin' crawl over his desk to get to the other side. Maybe Mackenzie would help me organize the place a bit, even put up a couple of her paintings.

I smiled, not just at my thought, but at the fact I was even having the thought at all. Damn, a lot had changed in a few short days. I had gone from feeling a bit sorry for myself to realizing my life was less important than at least one other person's in the world.

"Why are you smiling? This is taking forever," Denise said.

"Just thinking about stuff."

Yells of frustration from behind us, and the pair of assholes got their shit together and hurried off the plane.

Movement at last. As we finally made our way into the land of cleaner air, I glanced at the other text, the one from Nicole.

Hi, Oz. I talked to your brother. Sounds like you heard some big news. I'm excited for you, but also hoping you're doing okay. I miss hearing your voice, feeling your body against mine. Please let me know how things are going and when you'll be back in Austin. Lots to discuss.

Nicole xoxo

Ah, Tobin. My little brother just couldn't keep his mouth shut. The familiar pang of wanting Nicole with all my heart conflicted with the pain of what she'd put me through. Sure, focusing on Mackenzie and Denise had threatened my life, but it had served as a needed distraction as well.

Austin. The land of unfinished business. I typed in a quick reply.

Thanks for asking. Hanging in there. Long story, but hope to be back soon.

Take care,

Oz

I released a heavy sigh, but I was happy with my response. I couldn't completely resist the pull to Nicole, but I also couldn't pretend that nothing had happened. What she'd done to me, to our relationship, to innocent people, weren't things that could be easily forgotten. The last thing I wanted to do was jump back in bed with her—literally and figuratively—and then resent her for the rest of our lives.

"Is that your wife?"

I realized we were standing in the middle of a busy walkway outside of the gate. Apparently, I'd been in a daze. "How'd you know?"

"I could see it in your eyes."

"Didn't know my eyes could talk." I motioned for her to follow me. I spotted a sign for rental cars and made our way down an escalator. There, I signed a bunch of papers, and we headed outside to our car. It was snowing.

I couldn't make this shit up.

"Fuck!" Denise said, dropping her bag on the concrete just behind our car, a generic blue Buick.

I would have suggested that she calm down, but I knew that would incite a strong reaction. It was just human nature.

"We'll take it nice and slow," I said, opening the car, tossing in two duffel bags.

I started up the car, turned on the defroster and windshield wipers. Even I could hear the crunching scrape of the wipers against the frozen snow. Fortunately, the car-rental company had included an ice scraper in our "bronze" package. I got out, scraped a bit, then jumped back in the car.

"Your headlights are showing," Denise said.

I looked down at my chest. She was right. "You're full of humor."

"Just drive. But don't kill us please."

The roads weren't too bad. Barely half an inch of snow on the roads. And, unlike drivers in Texas, where any hint of moisture, frozen or not, created a massive freak-out, those on the East Coast were more accustomed to weather issues. They seemed to just deal with it and move on.

Traffic out of DC, even at the late hour, was slow. Too many cars, not enough roads. The pace picked up once we finally got out of the beltway and headed west on I-66. The flakes increased in size the farther we traveled.

"According to weather.com, there's four inches on the ground just across the border," Denise said.

"Let's find a town near the Camp Israel location and try to make it there tonight."

Denise kept busy—that was always a good thing. I got lost in my thoughts while driving in the heavy snowfall. Initially, I tried to picture seeing Mackenzie for the first time, imagining what I'd feel. What she would feel...if anything at all.

While I tried to avoid it, my thoughts shifted into a flood of questions. How, exactly, would we find Mackenzie? Would there be someone standing at this abandoned camp once we showed up, giving us an ovation for figuring out the answer to this riddle? And then the kidnapper would simply pat Mackenzie on the back and hand her over? My sarcastic imagination only showed me that I couldn't envision how this would work. Maybe that was the point—keep us guessing right until the end.

There had to be more of a motivation than simply seeing us solve the riddle. That seemed far too simplistic. And it didn't fit with how a crime syndicate might operate.

Which, for the umpteenth time, made me rethink who might be behind this.

Too many questions, too little time, and, most importantly, no one with any definitive answers.

We kept our talking to a minimum and stayed just below the speed limit. Denise said we should strive to make it to Elkins, the only town anywhere near the Camp Israel location, and it had a motel. One.

It was still snowing when we rolled into Elkins. The tallest structure in town first caught my gaze. Just off the town square sat a picturesque church. White snow covered rooftops and tree limbs. It seemed like a quaint town, like something I might see in one of Tito's Christmas paintings, even if I didn't spot a single human or moving vehicle.

Denise said, "Cute, but does anyone live here?" Two seconds later, I saw flashing blue and red lights in my rearview. I didn't have a good feeling about our welcome committee.

Twenty-One

Looking through my side mirror, I watched the local cop pull his heavyset body out of his police cruiser and plod through the thick snow. Looked more like six inches than four.

"What do you think he wants, Oz?" Denise snapped her head to look out the back window, a puzzled look on her face, and put a hand on my arm. "We weren't speeding. Hell, we were barely moving ten miles per hour."

"Nothing to worry about. It's a small town. I'm sure he just wants to make sure we're not Bonnie and Clyde."

I punched down the window.

"Hands on the steering wheel, boy."

Boy? I did as he said and withheld a verbal jab.

The officer reset his wide-brimmed hat that was covered with clear plastic, leaned down to peek across the front of the car. He had a toothpick on the left side of his mouth. He, who must have been close to my height of six-three, wore a thick jacket over his uniform, the kind that buttoned right at the waist. It wasn't a good look for a man with a monster-truck tire attached to his midsection.

Denise waved with her fingers.

"Ma'am, just to make me comfortable, I'm going to ask you put your hands on the dashboard."

"But why is—"

"Just do it, please," I said to her.

"There you go," the officer said. "Listen to your husband, darlin'."

"I'm not—"

"Denise," I said, giving her the eye, "please let the officer do his job. And then we can move on." I wasn't trying to be an ass to Denise, but I'd been around a few hick cops in my life. If you fell into the trap of verbally sparring with the officer, it almost always ended up poorly. I once saw two buddies handcuffed and taken to jail for just a couple of comebacks when the cop asked them to stand in a field while it was raining.

Denise clenched her jaw.

"I'm the sheriff of Elkins. Sheriff Tom Kupchak," he said, as his breath pumped white smoke into the air. "We usually have a quiet town, no outsiders. Well, except for the country craft fair. That brings in all the creative hippies. Just walk around the square, and you can smell marijuana."

Here we go. Telling us his life story. I nodded, kept my mouth shut, and, thankfully, Denise didn't offer any commentary either.

He asked for my license and proof of insurance. I asked if it was okay if I pulled out my wallet. He agreed, and I handed him the two cards, which he studied for a few seconds.

"We're using a rental car. Denise can show you the paperwork that's in the glove compartment."

"Sure, but be slow and easy about it. I want to make sure you're not hiding a gun in your car."

Denise twisted her face into a prune.

"Got a problem with that?" the sheriff barked, sticking his head in my window. His breath smelled of meatloaf and maybe fish. I stopped taking in air.

"No...sir." She unlatched the glove compartment and handed me the envelope, which I passed on to Sheriff Tom Kupchak.

He didn't even open it. "I knew you were a rental the first moment I saw you pass Peggy's Diner just outside of town."

I wanted to ask why anyone would eat meatloaf and fish in the same meal, but I withheld the urge to say anything.

"So do I need to give you two a breathalyzer?"

This coming from a man who smelled like he had a week-old flounder stuffed in his pocket.

"No sir. We haven't had a drink all day," I said, my voice even.

"So what are you doing in Elkins? Passing through, or do you have business here?"

"We want to know how to get to some place called Camp Israel," Denise blurted out.

I stared at her with eyes as big as plates.

"You want to do *what?*" Now the sheriff had his hands on his knees as he stared at her. He tipped his hat back, a look of confusion and ridicule washing over his face.

"It's not anything," I said with as much nonchalance as I could muster. I'd give him so much information he'd beg me to drive on. "She was just wondering about this camp. We stumbled on this news story when we were driving into town and were just curious." I paused for a second. He hadn't interrupted, so I continued with my epic sleep-inducing story. "So, we're just passing through. We flew into DC; you know Dulles? It's crowded as hell in DC. Too many people. I wanted to show her where I went to law school."

"Law school?" His voice jumped an octave. "You're one of them lawyers?"

Crap. I hit a hot button.

"Well, I used to be. The firm I worked at was shut down. So, I'm taking some time off and traveling across the country. We're on our way back to Texas. Just love hitting these quaint towns."

He nodded, chewed on his toothpick like it was cud. In fact, I believed he was part cow, which meant he would have eaten himself for dinner. Disgusting no matter how you wanted to look at it.

"Come to think of it, my sister-in-law sells souvenirs at her shop just around the corner. She even has some leftover shot glasses that have a picture of that Camp Israel compound on it. If you ask me, that's not very classy, but it makes her a few bucks. They were real popular here a few months ago. Not so much during the winter months."

"Well," I said, allowing a warm, nonthreatening smile to come to my lips. "We'll have to check that out tomorrow morning. Right, Denise?"

"Right, Ozzie."

"So, if everything is okay, we'll just go over and check into our—"

"That was a dark time in this community." The sheriff lifted to a standing position and tugged his sagging pants up higher. His eyes squinted as he stared into the snow-filled sky.

I wanted to grab the legal documents out of his hands and punch the gas, but I knew he'd probably have ten self-deputized peons hunting us down within minutes. So I just had to listen.

"I'm a religious guy, don't get me wrong," he said, glancing back in the car as if he were waiting on us to pump our fists.

"Amen." Man, I sounded cheesy.

"I know a good Christian when I see one," he said, handing me back the paperwork.

Christian, Jew. Same thing, right? Whatever.

"But some of that shit…uh, forgive me, Lord. Some of that crap they were doing up there in the hills," he said with a finger pointed north, "that was just sick. Perverted. Twisted. And on top of that, they were a bunch of no-good swindlers, trying to cheat hard-working people out of their money. Just a shame what some people do in the name of religion."

Finally, something we could agree on.

He cupped his hands, blew warm air into them. He was getting cold. I could taste victory, which was quite a feat, considering the wafts of greasy food in our space.

"Well, you enjoy your stay in Elkins, now." He tipped his cap. "Just remember that Peggy's Souvenir Shop opens at eight in the morning. She's never late."

"Peggy's. Right." I tapped a finger against my temple.

He got in his car and flipped off his flashing lights. I looked at Denise. "Where's the motel?"

Twenty-Two

The motel manager said all of three words when we checked in. "Need working heat?" He chewed on the end of his pen while I waited for the rest of the joke. It never came.

Denise was over at the window, watching a group of folks get out of a car and climb a flight of outdoor stairs. When I turned back around, the manager appeared to be picking food from his teeth with the pen.

"Yes, heat would be good on a night like tonight," I said.

He put a clipboard in front of me, pointed to the piece of paper, and then held the pen in front of my face. I looked across the counter that was peeling at the edges. "Do you have another pen?"

He shrugged and dipped his head at the same time. A man of many words. Using just two fingers to hold the pen, I signed my name and then quickly stuck my hand in my jeans pocket. We got a key to room 214, grabbed our bags, and carefully made our way up the slick steps. Once we reached the second floor, I looked to the left and saw the steeple of the church. It appeared to be the tallest building as far as the eye could see, which wasn't very far, considering it was the middle of the night and snowing.

I flipped around, and a door to another room had just opened. A woman walked out with an empty ice bucket. She had a blank look on her face, catatonic almost. She walked by us. I noticed Denise was staring inside the open room. I took a single step back and looked inside for myself. A guy was sniffing something up his nose off a glass table. It had to be coke. I saw four other people, including one who was wrapping his upper arm with a large rubber band.

"Come on, Denise." I headed off toward our room. When I didn't see her pull up next to me, I turned around again. She was still at that doorway. She looked like a dog salivating over a steak. And it made my mouth go dry. I retraced my steps and then nudged her arm. "Something wrong?"

"Oh…" Her eyes darted about. It was as if she'd forgotten where she was, or that we were standing outside in freezing temperatures. "I'm fine." Her voice sounded hollow.

As we made our way toward room 214, I saw her sneak another glance down the hall. I shut the door, hoping to shut down her demons along with it, and we unpacked our things. Thankfully, the room had two queen beds. We agreed to figure out the exact location of this Camp Israel compound in the morning, which was all of four hours away. We traded a little small talk, and then I dozed off.

The moment my eyes opened, I pulled up, looked at the other bed.

No Denise.

Crap.

I threw the covers, walked to the door.

"You looking for me?"

I turned to see Denise sitting on the bathroom counter, smoking a cigarette.

"I didn't know you smoked."

"I'm a mysterious girl, what can I say?" Her eyes looked heavy. She leaned against the sink. "I only smoke when I'm stressed."

"Are you stressed from Mackenzie being kidnapped?" I paused, looking for any acknowledgement. I saw nothing, so I continued my thought. "Or could you be stressed by the lure of what we saw going on in the room down the way?"

"You don't beat around the bush, do you?"

Her leg was kicking like a little kid sitting in a high chair.

"We've come this far. I think we need to be honest with each other."

"Honest. I guess that's your way of saying you think I'm about to break my sobriety and go off the deep end."

I took two steps toward her, but, despite the billowing smoke in the room, I could still see her face. She wasn't in the mood for a hug.

"Look, Denise, I just know you're under stress that very few people have ever experienced. And you've been amazing. Sure, you've been emotional, but who wouldn't be? You've picked yourself up and taken action." I choked out a breath, then waved the smoke away from my face. "You had your life threatened, Mackenzie's life threatened, we've been assaulted, and now we're chasing down the answer to this riddle, hoping and praying that Mackenzie is at the end of this thing. I mean, few people could even imagine this kind of shit. For you to be able to sit here and be functioning at all is remarkable."

She took a drag on her cigarette, pushed the smoke out the side of her mouth, and stared at me a few seconds before looking off.

I let a few seconds pass. Her leg kept kicking, but the cigarette remained at her side, her eyes heavy.

"I believe in you, Denise. I know you've been through some shit in your life. A lot of shit. It's part of your past. I just want to help support you to ensure it remains part of your past."

She dropped the cigarette in the sink, her face still vacant, and walked toward me. I leaned back a bit. Was she about to slap me?

"Dammit, Ozzie," she said, a couple of feet in front of me. She thumped my chest, then grabbed me by the shoulders and hugged me. It literally took my breath away. I had no idea she had that kind of energy. Although I knew she had that kind of passion, especially for Mackenzie.

I put my hand on the back of her head. "It will be okay, Denise. We'll get through this together."

"With Mackenzie." She didn't say that as a question, like she might have a couple of days prior. She was telling me. She held me tight and long. We rocked back and forth. I couldn't hear any sobs. But I could feel her will—to remain resolute in keeping her life together, in finding her child. Our child.

Just then, a piercing sound split the silence. It felt like a high-pitched siren had gone off in my head. I put both hands against my ears, but I couldn't stop the reverberation. It was dizzying, nauseating even. I squeezed my eyes shut. My ear drums were about to explode. There was movement around me, through the smoke.

"What…?" I started to ask as I opened my eyes to see Denise on top of the bed, a shoe in hand.

My eyes shifted to the fire alarm. It was flashing red.

Of course, it was the alarm, stupid.

She rammed the heel of her shoe into the alarm, sending fragments of plastic flying through the air like mini-shrapnel.

The spring of the mattress made Denise sway up and down, but other than that, she wasn't moving. Neither was I.

"Quiet," she whispered.

I still heard a distant ring in my ear, but the feeling of a knife being stabbed into my ear had, thankfully, gone away.

"You're badass," I said, trying to give her a morale boost.

"Actually, I'm a dumbass for smoking in this lovely establishment." She climbed off the bed, tossed her shoe in the corner. "Do you think the manager will kick us out?"

"Who knows if there's even a manager still at the front desk? I think we're more likely to see Wonder Woman show up outside our door than the manager."

She arched her eyebrow. "Sounds like you had some fun dreams."

"Uh…" I fumbled my words, not sure what to say. I didn't recall any of my dreams, let alone about Wonder Woman.

"You don't have to say anything," she said with a wink.

With the intensity back to a livable level, she washed her face while I changed into my jeans. We pulled out our phones, opened up our map apps, and identified the location of Camp Israel in relation to where we were. The route to get there would take us through a small town called Parsons up in the mountains. From there, the camp appeared to be another twenty minutes or so to the southeast, snaking through some narrow roads that might still be covered in snow. As for the compound itself, unfortunately Google Earth didn't show much other than the tops of two buildings. It appeared that the pictures had been taken in the spring, when the surrounding foliage was thickest.

"This place is in the middle of the woods," Denise said.

"Looks that way," I said, scratching my chin. I hadn't shaved in days.

I shifted the view to the right and pointed out what looked like a barn and a fence behind the buildings as the elevation increased.

"Rough terrain. Tons of trees, boulders," Denise said.

Moving to the other side of the building, I spotted what looked like a narrow dirt road. I lost the visual while shifting farther east, but then after about a mile, I saw what I assumed was the same dirt road emptying onto a narrow highway.

"I think there's some type of fence with a gate near the road," I said.

We wondered how big the complex was. It was impossible to see through the maps.

"I think I need to ask some folks around town," I said as I put on my shoes and tied them. I'd brought only running shoes. Hiking boots would have been better, but I'd deal with that while in town.

I noticed it was after eight o'clock. "How about I go get some breakfast, ask a few questions along the way in the most unassuming way possible, and then I'll come back and we can figure out a plan?"

"I'm not a fan of the cold anyway," she said, giving me a pat on the arm. "I might even take a shower, just to get some of this grime off me."

I walked to the door. She ran up, gave me a kiss on the cheek. "Thank you again, Ozzie."

"Of course. We're in this together, right?"

"You got it. I was thinking…while you're out scouting, see if you can find a place that has coats and boots. Might need them for later."

I gave her a wink and headed off.

Twenty-Three

The snow had stopped, but the skies were gunmetal gray. A few cars were actually on the road, moving at a slow but steady pace. Only a handful of folks walking about town. I wasn't sure what percentage of the population that represented.

I circled the square, my eyes continuously diverting to the big church. I saw an older woman walk inside. Looking back to the road, a line of folks were huddled together, talking and drinking coffee outside of a place called Fred's Donuts.

That had to be the morning social-gathering place. I found an empty spot around the town square, then boogied across the snow and up on the sidewalk.

"Out of towner." A guy with skin that sagged like a mastiff's shifted his head out from a group of guys.

Rather obvious, Einstein. I was wearing a short-sleeved button-up shirt. I nodded and blew warm air into my hands.

"People just have no sense, you know what I mean, Darryl?" Mastiff Man had said the words under his breath, but I could read lips. One of the advantages to not being able to hear worth a lick.

I ignored him and walked inside. It was warmer…maybe a balmy sixty. I waited in line behind two women. Both of them took turns looking at me, rolling their eyes. I was starting to get the impression they all thought I'd escaped the nearest psych ward—which didn't seem like that much of a stretch—or they were freaked out by my presence just because I wasn't one of them.

Disarming. That was my go-to strategy.

"How are you ladies doing this chilly morning?"

"Pretty good, pretty good," a woman with pink cheeks and pinker head scarf nodded. I thought I saw a slight smile.

"Carol, there's no need…" The other woman, who had on earrings with "WVA" engraved on them, turned away from me, shaking her head.

"I know you must think I'm a little crazy with no coat in this part of the country."

"Kind of, yes," Carol said, with only a quick glance my way.

I said, "Me and my girlfriend….uh, I mean, my wife…were just driving across the country, from DC down to Texas. This seemed like a cute town to stop in for the night."

"Don't they wear coats up in DC?" The woman with the WVA earrings apparently hadn't stopped listening. Before I could respond, she continued. "Actually, I'm not sure anyone has the sense in that city to know when to get in from the rain." She giggled, which sounded like a seal. I laughed and looked at Carol, who also laughed.

"Oh, Betty, you and your laugh," Carol said. They laughed some more, and so did I.

I think we just had our first bonding moment.

I looked at the menu on the wall above the front counter. It was one of those boards where the red plastic letters were pressed into a white grid to spell out their menu items. About twenty or so types of donuts, although there was at least one letter missing from almost every type of donut. They also had kolaches, although the board was missing the "o."

"You can see that Fred's is the most popular place in town," Carol said, looking over my shoulder. I followed her gaze to see about ten people behind me. She actually stuck out her hand and touched my forearm. She was a toucher.

"Why is that?" I asked.

"Well, for starters," Betty said, leaning in closer, "Fred Willard worships money more than the Good Lord above."

I gave a slow nod. Carol turned her shoulders, as if she were trying to block anyone from seeing or hearing her friend.

"He basically shut down two other donut shops," Betty said. Her earrings shook nonstop for a few seconds after she nodded.

"How could he do that?"

"He's on the planning and zoning commission," Carol whispered. "He's almost like…" Her beady eyes darted around before settling on me. "Now don't laugh or anything. But he thinks he's the Godfather or something."

As she suggested, I tried not to laugh. In fact, I tried to show off whatever scowl I could muster.

"We're not kidding," Carol said. "Somehow he pushed through—"

"*Bribed* is probably more like it," Betty said, her jaw suddenly stiff.

Carol nodded toward her friend. "Maybe. Probably. But he persuaded the rest of the commission to basically change the zoning for two other rival businesses after they'd already been open."

I stuck a hand in my pocket, tried to look interested. I was sure this gossip created quite the buzz. To me, it was petty, small-town politics. And certainly nothing that would help me learn more about Camp Israel and finding Mackenzie.

The people in front of us were taking forever to order, so I took the opportunity to pivot the conversation.

"Are you a fan of the Mountaineers?" I asked Betty. "Lovely earrings, by the way."

She tilted her head, put a hand to her ear. "These were a gift from my son, Earl. He went to school at WVA, and he gave these to me as a gift when he graduated."

"Very nice of him to take care of his mom."

"Did you know he's actually a bit of a local hero?" Carol asked, touching my arm again.

"Oh, Carol, you don't have to brag about Earl." Betty tried to sound modest, but it had the opposite effect.

"Now you have me really intrigued," I said.

"Earl works in the sheriff's department in Kanawha County. That's the largest county in the entire state."

A single nod, waiting for more. Hoping for more.

"Well, about a year ago or so—"

Betty interrupted. "It was actually more like fifteen months, if you want to be exact, Carol."

"Okay, fifteen months ago, Earl helped take down the most vile set of criminals this state has ever seen." Hand on my arm again.

"Police put their lives on the line every day. It's a tough job," I said.

"Well, he was exactly in the direct line of fire," Betty said.

"True," her friend agreed. "But he was on the scene during the original FBI bust on that Camp Israel."

I felt the blood drain from my face. "I think I read something about that. He was involved, huh?"

"Like I said. He didn't get shot at. But he was there within a couple of hours. He worked right alongside the FBI, and he helped those poor people, who were essentially held hostage in that compound. A couple of religious zealots were running that place, brutalizing women, even young girls. It was just the most awful thing. In fact, they had planned on killing most of the remaining people on the compound had it not been for a couple of FBI agents who stormed the place."

I could feel my palms go sweaty, and I pulled them from my pockets. "That's an amazing story. And Betty, you should feel very proud of your son."

"Thank you..."

"Ozzie."

"Ozzie." She pronounced the syllables as if she were in the first grade. "Well, Earl hasn't told his boss yet, but he has hopes of applying to get into the FBI Academy in Quantico, Virginia."

"I'm sure he'd make a fine federal agent."

We made it to the front of the line. The only options were the ones lined with grease and fat. I purchased half a dozen kolaches and two coffees.

"Well, Ozzie, it was so nice meeting you. You seem like a nice young man," Carol said at the door as she slipped on her gloves. "Did you say you had a girlfriend or wife?"

I'd slipped up on that earlier. But I'd told the sheriff she was my wife. Better to stick with one story, since the town was so small.

"We actually just got married."

"Well, how exciting. Are you two thinking of kids?"

I could feel my chest tighten. "It's come up in conversation recently," I said with a smile.

They started to walk out. This time, I touched Betty's arm. "My wife and I are real explorers and very curious. About how long would it take us to drive to this compound and check it out?"

"Oh, I get what you mean. It's like those ax murders a dozen years ago. Everyone who came through town wanted to see where these horrible crimes took place. So, we know lots of people who go out to Camp Israel. From what I understand, they have the whole perimeter locked down. And it's basically abandoned. Not sure what the government will do with fifty acres out on the side of a mountain."

"Locked down, huh?"

"Well, between you and me, Earl said the easiest way to get in there and really see the buildings and such is to enter on the northeast side. There's a fence, but you can scale it."

"Maybe we'll just take a few pictures," I said.

I pushed open the door, and we all walked outside. The blustery wind bit into my exposed skin.

"There's Peggy's Apparel around the corner," Carol said, pointing over my shoulder. "You do any hiking in these parts and you'll freeze your little acorns off." She giggled, and Betty did her seal impression.

I waved goodbye and scooted toward the car.

Twenty-Four

My phone buzzed as I juggled two coffees and the box of kolaches, trying not to slip on the snow while opening the car door. If Sheriff Tom Kupchak had seen that graceful act, he probably would have hauled me off to jail for public intoxication or some other fictional charge.

Once inside the car—my hands now soaked with coffee—I saw that I'd missed a call from Brook, my detective friend from the Austin police force. I turned on the car, cranked the heat, and called her back.

"You're alive."

"That's quite a greeting. Hello to you too," I said, searching the car for a napkin to wipe my hands.

"I didn't know what was going on. You kind of left me hanging after your frantic call the other night."

"I've been…busy."

"With what? Wait, don't bother with all that right now. Just tell me that you have your daughter, Mackenzie."

A sigh. "No. Not yet. We have hope, though. I just wonder if it's false hope at this point."

"From what I know of you, Oz, you're usually not one to speak in such vague terms."

I found a napkin, cleaned off my hands, and rubbed my eyes. A weariness had settled in. I'd been masking it with occasional bursts of adrenaline. At the moment, my brain didn't have the capability to parse through what I should or shouldn't share with Brook. After all, she was a law-enforcement officer.

"Look, we're following this lead that was given to us at Denise's apartment."

"How promising is it?"

"Promising. Well, it was given to us in the form of a riddle."

"You mean like Batman and Robin?"

"I wish I could laugh. Kind of, yes."

She asked for the content of the note, and I recited it to her. I heard a sigh, and maybe an under-the-breath string of cuss words, but I wasn't sure. And I didn't really care.

She asked my opinion on the *yakuza*'s involvement.

"Who the hell knows at this point? Keo, at first, had his suspicions. And then his friend, Humala, spoke to her *yakuza* contact. He denied it but, again, didn't rule out the possibility of some splinter group acting irrationally and doing its own thing. But sitting here with snow all around me in the middle of the hills of West Virginia, it's—"

"You're where?"

"Oh. I forgot to tell you how we solved the riddle. Or at least we think we did."

I briefly walked her through our thought process for the three pieces of the riddle. I didn't hear anything for a few seconds. I felt behind my ear and made sure my hearing aid was turned up. It was.

"Are you still there, Brook?"

"I'm thinking. Your logic, more or less, makes sense. But this could all be a farce, just to get you to run across the country when Mackenzie is still in Hawaii."

A pang of unease took hold of my gut. Part of me wanted to lash out at someone, and right now Brook was the easy choice. I picked up one of the coffees and sipped it, felt the heat slither down my chest. And then I took a deep breath. "What you said is possible. We had to make a decision. I wanted to go by myself and have Denise stay in Hawaii, but she insisted. Besides, I'd be worried for her safety if she wasn't with me. Then again, I was with her at her apartment when we were assaulted by a tank and guy with nunchucks."

That led to another debrief and ten more questions. I was beginning to feel like I was being interrogated, but I knew she meant well. Hell, she was one of the few people I trusted.

I put the car in reverse and slowly made my way out of the parking area.

"Any major injuries?" she asked after a few seconds.

"A few bumps and cuts. A normal day at the office, at least in the last week or two."

"Damn, you've been put through hell. So, here's the thing, Oz. I think we might want to take a step back and reassess how you….we move forward on this thing."

"We?"

"That's right, I said 'we.' You and Denise are not in this alone. You can't be."

Her direct nature was actually helping, making me feel like someone in this world gave a damn.

"I'm listening," I said.

"This Camp Israel place…I'm familiar with that story and all the crazy shit that went on there. Stan and I—when I worked in San Antonio—talked about it extensively. Did you know his cousin, Nick, the one with the FBI, was on the scene, actually saved dozens of lives?"

"You're the second person today to tell me they know someone who saved the world at this compound."

"I'm not bullshitting you, Oz. Nick was there. He got shot. These nutjob religious leaders were going to gas their flock of followers like some type of Nazi concentration-camp gas chamber."

She got my attention, only because Nick's involvement sounded much closer to the action than that of Betty's son. I knew Stan, at least a bit. My mind suddenly became overwhelmed with colliding data points. Or was it something else? Whatever. It was just damn surreal to have this third degree of separation with a location where so much harm had taken place. I wasn't really sure how to process it. For now, it just lingered, along with all the other crap I couldn't make sense of.

"Okay, I'm impressed. So what does that mean?"

"Could they—and we have no idea who *they* are or why *they* took Mackenzie or even if it's some *yakuza* splinter group—be holding Mackenzie somewhere on this compound in the middle of the West Virginia wilderness? Yes, it's possible. But sane, rational people… Let me rephrase that. People like the *yakuza* are typically more focused on the impact to their business. They have a goal in mind. Playing jokes like this—"

"Technically, it's a riddle."

"Okay. This riddle doesn't sound like a characteristic I'd associate with that crime syndicate. I know I'm not the world's leading authority on how they operate. It's just my opinion, based on what I know."

I stopped at a light behind a truck with a Doberman in the back. I instantly flashed back to the night when Nicole's dog essentially saved our lives. It was the night she'd finally let her guard down, opened up, and told me how sorry she was for going off the rails. Even in the middle of this cross-country quest to find a daughter I never knew existed, I could still feel the pull of Nicole. Her text when we were at LAX confirmed she was still remorseful and trying to be supportive. Could I get past all of her indiscretions to even think about piecing together our relationship? I pushed it aside for now, although my brain was beginning to feel like Ray Gartner's office—crammed with so much shit, it was almost impossible to operate.

"Houston, do you read me?"

"Sorry, I was just focused on some local traffic." The light turned green, and the truck with the dog in the back turned right. I moved forward.

"So Ozzie, please hear me on this. With everything you've told me about what happened on the Big Island, I think you need help. You can't keep going at this alone."

"Denise is with me."

"I already know about her issues."

"Low blow, Brook."

"It's true, though. But that doesn't really matter. She's got skin in the game. So do you. You're not law enforcement."

"I got to know the sheriff of this little town when we first arrived. Interesting guy." I traveled two more blocks, then turned left. I saw Peggy's Souvenir Shop, just like Sheriff Kupchak had noted. Next to that was Peggy's Apparel. I recalled the sheriff saying he'd been at Peggy's Diner. Maybe Peggy and this Fred Willard donut guy were like the Google and Facebook of Elkins. Bitter business rivals unless they could both benefit from a situation.

"So, I know what you're going to say, Brook. Call in the cops; let them take care of it. But I can't. Denise won't let me. They said they'd…" A lump formed in my throat. I sipped some coffee and continued. "They said they'd kill Mackenzie. If that happened, Denise would shatter into a million pieces. There would be nothing left of her. As for me, I've come this far, Brook. I want to get to know my daughter, to see if she cares two cents about me. To see how we're alike, how we're different."

"I get it."

I felt my shoulders drop. "Good, because I don't need another battle."

"But that doesn't mean I agree. Just hear me out. Cops...you're right. Keep them out of it. Hawaii cops could be connected to the *yakuza*. The local cops there in BFE, West Virginia, would probably do more harm than good. But we have Stan. He can get Nick on the phone in an instant. He told me as much."

"You've talked to him about this situation?"

"Sure have. It's just between us. That was before I knew all this other crap had taken place. I'm telling you, Oz. Let him call Nick. I can be on the line too. He will maintain discretion; I can almost guarantee it. And if, after that conversation, you decide to still be bullheaded, then I guess there's nothing we can do."

I drove into the motel parking lot and parked the car. "Let me get back to you on that."

"Don't take long, Ozzie. We want to help. Nick, according to Stan, is one of the best agents in the FBI. He understands the importance of family. He won't ram a bunch of protocol down your throat."

I thanked her, and we ended our call.

I grabbed the breakfast and two coffees and made my way up the steps. No surprise, the manager had yet to clean off the snow or add salt or sand. Halfway down the hall to our motel room, my phone buzzed again.

Crap. I didn't want Denise to be aware of the possibility of calling Nick, an FBI agent, to assist us. She might lose it on me. I set one of the coffees on the concrete and pulled out my phone. It was a text from Keo.

I read it, and then I could hardly breathe.

Twenty-Five

A motel door opened in front of me. The only thing I noticed about the person who trudged by me was that he or she was shorter and walking on two legs. I reread the text from Keo.

Police found Gwen Hammond dead in her back yard. Strangulation. Police buddy of mine says a neighbor might have seen someone, but I have no details yet.

I went from barely breathing to my brain being flooded with oxygen.

Gwen, Denise's friend, the person who'd allowed us to stay the night after we'd been attacked in Denise's apartment, had been fucking murdered. I blinked my eyes a few times. A breeze crossed my face, but it didn't feel cold. I didn't feel much of anything.

I typed in a response.

Have you sent a message to Denise yet?

A moment later, he came back with his reply.

No way. Wanted to tell u first. Police will start asking questions. Not sure if they'll find out about Mackenzie's kidnapping or Denise threatening to expose yakuza *crimes.*

Up to this point, I'd been able to somehow deal with all the craziness. But someone had now been murdered. That someone was Denise's best friend. Surely, authorities would learn of their connection, which would only lead to more questions. With the blur of the new facts almost making my eyes water, it was impossible to determine whether that was good or bad. Or did it really matter? We didn't want to create more conflict with this crime syndicate or with whatever splinter group that might have been born from it. But the more I learned, the more confused I became.

Killing Gwen, to a degree, made sense if the *yakuza* thought Denise had shared with her the money-laundering details. But something about it didn't ring true. I racked my brain for answers, but nothing stuck. I just couldn't put my finger on why part of my instinct was telling me the *yakuza* had nothing to do with any of this.

Then explain this, Oz: why the hell did two Asian guys bust into Denise's apartment and beat the crap out of you?

I pushed out a breath and saw smoke drift into the air. That same person walked back by me again and went into their room without saying a word. At least this time I noticed it was a man, maybe upper forties. Wearing hunting gear.

I got back to my text conversation with Keo.

Me: *I'm assuming no one has dropped off any other notes about Mackenzie?*

Keo: *Nope. All quiet here.*

Me: *Can you let me know if or when you find out more information about Gwen?*

Keo: *Sure thing. Are you going to tell Denise?*

I thought about that for a second.

Me: *I'm not sure. I don't want her to fall apart, or get more scared for herself or Mackenzie.*

Keo: *There is a possibility that this murder may not be related. Hawaii is not immune to crime.*

Me: *Possibly. But likely?*

Keo: *My gut tells me it's related. How, though? To me, it seems too messy to be related to yakuza. Strangulation? They found her body in the back yard. There was an eyewitness. Sounds almost amateur…maybe an act of passion. I wonder if Gwen had any ex-boyfriends, or maybe a stalker???*

Me: *Interesting points. I don't know those answers. Denise might, so there's another reason the cops will want to talk to her.*

Keo: *Might be twenty-four hours or less before they get to Denise.*

Me: *I want to take action on this end before they reach out to Denise. Keep me informed please.*

Keo: *Roger that.*

I began to feel the cold bite into my skin. It seemed I'd dealt with this latest blow and come back to earth. I was about to slip the phone into my pocket when it buzzed again.

Keo: *U never told me where things stand. Any closer to finding Mackenzie?*

I looked out, off into the distance. The thick clouds had lightened a bit. I could make out a few rolling hills, tree-covered limbs.

Me: *Not yet. We're thinking she might be in a certain location just north of us. Headed that way shortly.*

Keo: *Be careful. Bringing a weapon?*

Damn. I hadn't even thought about it.

Me: *Not sure. Will first need to buy a coat.*

Keo: *Don't know what those are. Send me a picture. Hawaiian humor.:)*

Me: *Will do. Later.*

Keo: *Maika'i pōmaika'i!*

Me: *Need a translation??*

Keo: *Good luck, my friend.*

Me: *Thx*

I grabbed the two cold coffees and the bag of breakfast food. Walking toward our motel room, I was unsure how to approach any of this with Denise.

Twenty-Six

The coffee was cold, and the kolaches were cold. I apologized to Denise, and we threw the food away. We grabbed some crackers and soft drinks out of the vending machines downstairs and ate in the car.

Sitting in the motel parking lot, we actually made a bit of small talk, discussing the advantages of living in a small town and how raising kids in an environment like that might be different than in a big city or even the suburbs. We talked about the pressures of kids growing up in a society with so much technology at their fingertips...the power and enticement that was never more than a click away.

Yes, that made us both think of Mackenzie. Denise said that Mackenzie, like most kids, was enthralled with devices and their infinite access to information—not all of it factual, of course. We talked about how she'd be ten years old in a few months, and from there, her teenager life would soon follow. I could hear Denise's regret for not being the kind of parent she'd wanted to be. I only offered hope. There would be so many more opportunities to care for and love Mackenzie, to shape her life, to be there when she was down or needed help with homework—especially in subjects like math. She laughed when I said that.

The one thing I didn't discuss with Denise was what I'd learned from Keo—that Gwen had been murdered. No way. Not now. If she hated me for it later, then so be it.

Our first stop was at Peggy's Apparel. Denise and I were fitted with hiking boots, jackets, gloves, and hats. It took about an hour and ran us north of five hundred dollars. Thank God Nicole had reopened access to my accounts. If it had been a week earlier, back when I barely had twenty bucks to my name, Denise and I would have been doing our best impression of Bonnie and Clyde. I knew if Nicole happened to be monitoring my charges, she might wonder why I was buying all of this winter gear in a small town in West Virginia. But I was rather certain she knew to let me do my thing without questioning my methods.

As they packaged up our gear, I noticed a pawn shop across the street. Fred's Pawn Shop. The business smackdown with Peggy continued.

I told Denise to wait inside Peggy's, that I'd be back in a few minutes. I quickly walked across the road. The bell dinged just above my head when I walked in. Two men were examining rifles near a counter against the far wall. I assumed they were not loaded with ammunition. "Can I hep ya?"

I flipped around and saw a guy who only had one tooth. No kidding. One. Single. Tooth. And his face looked like used sandpaper.

"Looking for a pistol." I swung my head around. I knew basically nothing about guns, other than a couple I'd seen presented in cases at the courthouse.

"Well, you've come to the right place." He walked like one leg was shorter than the other and got behind a small counter. "Hell, it's really the only place in Elkins to buy firearms and ammunition and a host of other weapons, depending on what you're huntin'."

I nodded, walked closer to the display case.

"So," he said with his palms flat on the glass, "what you huntin'?"

I looked up and studied his eyes. He seemed to be studying mine even more.

"Well..." I started walking and then mumbled something. I had no idea what was in season. I couldn't say, *"Oh, I'm hunting these lunatics who kidnapped my daughter, who I didn't know existed until just a few days ago."*

Yeah, I knew, even for this old-timer, that would get me nowhere. I'd be kicked out, and we'd be forced to search the compound with no weapon to protect us.

"Sorry, my hearing's a little off," he said, pulling up near me as he wiggled a finger in his ear. Didn't I know.

I glanced up and saw stuffed animals affixed to the side of the walls.

"Must be bobcat you huntin', huh?"

He'd followed my gaze.

I spotted his nametag. Oliver. Didn't really fit his look, but I went with it. "You're very observant, Oliver."

"Folks call me Ollie."

Bobcats? The thought that we might run into a bobcat made me question the whole plan, especially the part with Denise tagging along. "I think you just happened to catch me looking around." I shifted my sights to three stuffed animal heads. "I'm looking to have a little fun with something that's not as dangerous to my health."

"Ah, beaver. Good choice. We got a shitload o' beaver in these parts. Would do us some good to lower that population some."

"Cool."

Before I said another word, he'd laid out two rifles and three pistols on a board covered with red velvet, which looked like it had been pasted on by a preschooler. He showed his one-tooth smile, and I stepped forward and eyed each weapon. He then went through the pluses and minuses of each gun. He knew his stuff, without a doubt.

I didn't understand what he was talking about or really even cared, but I nodded plenty.

"Tough choice, ain't it?"

"I'm kind of stuck between this one," I put my had on one of the rifles, "and this one." I shifted my hand to the pistol with a grip that looked like it would fit my hand.

Without saying a word, one-tooth Ollie checked to make sure there was no ammo in it. Then he gave me the gun and told me to aim at a target at the opposite end of the store. He walked through a scenario of finding a beaver alongside a stream and then told me to pull the trigger. After we completed the exercise with both guns, I scratched my chin.

"You struggling with this choice, huh?"

"Well, Ollie, here's the deal. I got this chick across the street, and she said if I can prove to her that I'm a real man—and by that I mean killing one beaver or something like that within two hours—then she'll give me the best blowjob I could possibly imagine."

He froze.

I wondered if I'd taken it too far. I snapped my fingers in front of his face. He quaked back to attention. "Sorry, I was stuck on an old memory. But I wanna hep ya out. Problem is, background checks and all will take a while."

I leaned closer. "I'll give you a hundred-dollar tip if you submit the background check and just let me walk."

He narrowed his eyes so much it was hard to tell he had an iris. "You some mole brought in by the Feds, see if we're followin' the letter of the law?"

"Me? I hate the Feds. Just a waste of taxpayer money."

He nodded once, but he was back in study mode.

"Dude, I can bring the girl over, but then she'd know I don't know a whole lot about guns or hunting."

"So you're here strictly to get the girl to go down on you."

I shrugged. "I'm a guy. What can I say?"

"Make it two hundred."

"Deal."

He gave me ammunition for the Walther P22, packaged it up, and threw it into a backpack. Perfect. He opened the door for me on the way out.

"Good luck. Or should I say, 'good luck gettin' lucky'?"

I smirked and walked out. But I didn't cross the street to Peggy's. I walked to the car and got in. I opened the map app on my phone and studied it for a second; then I typed in a text to Denise.

Got done quicker than I thought. I'm off to get gas. I'll swing by in a few minutes.

I'd made it two blocks when she replied.

Why not take me? Whatever. Make it snappy. I'm getting itchy.

I huffed out a breath, knowing what I was about to do would piss her off to no end. I spotted a gas station and headed that way, but I didn't get gas for the car. I ran inside, found a packaged yellow raincoat—it was the only coat they had. My new cold-weather gear was still with Denise. I bought the raincoat, jumped back in the car, and took off. I reached the highway and headed north on 219.

Two minutes later, my phone rattled in the cup holder.

After wrestling with everything I'd learned from Keo and even Brook, I had made a unilateral decision back in the pawn shop. There was no way I was going to risk Denise's life on this mission. It wasn't as though she were trained in the martial arts. Ensuring she stayed out of harm's way, in my mind, would only take my focus away from finding Mackenzie. I didn't know if I'd walk into a gunfight or a fight with a bobcat. Or no fight at all. Really, I could trust only myself.

Brook, of course, would beg to differ. I thought long and hard about getting this Nick guy involved. But again, I couldn't take the risk. The kidnappers had been clear: if I brought in law enforcement, they'd kill Mackenzie.

I picked up the phone and read a string of cuss words in a text from Denise.

With one eye on the road, I typed in the following: *Sorry. I'll let you know when I have her.*

And then I shut off my phone and drove to Camp Israel.

Twenty-Seven

Buicks were not meant to be driven in the snow. Certainly not snowdrifts. I learned this the hard way. First, I approached the gate just off the main road to Camp Israel. I got out of my car, noticed the gate had multiple chains with padlocks, and surveyed the area, looking for a break in the fence. I thought I noticed such a break just beyond a row of thick trees. I got in my car, drove down about a hundred yards or so, and saw what looked like another dirt road covered by snow. I didn't see any tire tracks, but it had to be passable if it was an open path into the compound.

I was wrong. Big time. Not twenty feet off the main road, the car sank about four feet and didn't budge. I revved the engine, throwing it into reverse gear, and then back into drive. It barely moved an inch. I was screwed. I crawled through the window, trudged through the snow in my running shoes—all the winter gear was back with Denise at Peggy's Apparel, where she undoubtedly was so pissed she might have lit the place on fire. I made my way up to the tree line, pushed my way through thick foliage where mounds of snow fell inside my shirt, and found a barbed-wire fence. Not just any barbed-wire fence, but one that stood eight feet high and had that rolling razor wire you'd find on prison fences.

I didn't mind taking a few cuts to get to Mackenzie, but I also knew I'd be no good if I tried to climb over the fence and found my skin skewered by the barbed wire like a fly in a spider's web.

I retraced my steps and climbed onto the road, where there was only a thin layer of packed snow, and looked down to the main gate. I asked myself how the kidnappers would have entered the compound. There were no fresh tire tracks, and the place was on lockdown.

Betty and Carol, my besties from the donut shop, had said the Feds had seized the property. But I also recalled something else Betty had mentioned. Her son Earl had said there was a scalable fence on the northeast corner of the property.

Hmmm. I knew the property was about fifty acres. I glanced in a northeasterly direction, and all I could see were the snow-covered tips of trees. I had no choice. It was the only path I knew to take. I raced back to the car, pulled out my raincoat, stuck the pistol in my back waistband, and walked east along the road until the fence ended. I then plunged back into the deep snow and began the hike, moving north along the east side of the fence—my running shoes completely soaked. Within a couple of minutes, I couldn't feel my toes. The blanket of trees, however, did reduce the wind velocity.

Small victories.

In certain spots, the snow was above my waist, and I momentarily wondered what it would be like to find myself stuck in a snowdrift so deep that I suffocated. That thought only made my breathing more labored.

An hour or so into the hike, I thought I saw the northerly edge of the fence. I picked up my pace—it felt as though I was plodding on a pair of wooden stilts. Branches smacked against my face; it was so numb I hardly cared. I was almost there. I trudged forward, moved past a cluster of trees, and then stopped. The fence had not ended. It was still eight feet high and covered in razor wire. I momentarily considered trying to climb one of the many trees and do my own little high-wire act to reach the other side. But the type of trees just didn't give me that option. They were either tall and thin—so tall they looked like they touched the clouds—or they were evergreens, shaped like Christmas trees, with none of the branches strong enough to hold my weight.

Onward I marched. Thankfully, at the top of the second hill, I hit pay dirt—the end of the fence.

Again, small victories. Earl had been right. Just at the corner, there was a break in the fence. The wires had all been cut. They probably thought very few people would know to walk this far and stumble upon this opening. I turned sideways and slid through without a scrape.

I began moving west and slightly south. The snow wasn't as deep, and there were fewer trees, as if someone had spent some time clearing out the area. The wind had picked back up. I touched my face and realized I had snot frozen to my nose and cheeks. The wind chill must have been in the teens, and here I was, wearing a raincoat. A yellow one at that. If any type of sniper was searching for me, I'd be an easy target. Ollie might say, "Like shootin' ducks out of a barrel. And you'd be the dead duck."

As I moved closer, I considered ditching the raincoat. I could practically feel a laser target on my chest. The terrain sloped downward, and it felt like I was moving at a quicker pace.

Something bolted out from behind a tree. My heart nearly split my chest open, and I fell backward. I looked up and saw a deer— a damn big one. Thankfully, he ignored me. I felt the thud of his hooves through the frozen ground. And he disappeared off into the woods.

I got to my feet, brushed myself off. One heart attack avoided.

My eyes, every available sense, were on high alert, not just for Mackenzie or any other person, but also deer. Oh yeah, I couldn't forget about bobcats. I reached behind my back and touched the grip of the pistol. I considered holding the gun in my hand, but I didn't want to accidentally pull the trigger—that would give away my location. Maybe I'd consider it once I was closer. My running assumption was that they had her in one of the buildings I'd seen from the map app.

And not thirty seconds later, I saw the edge of the large L-shaped building. I hunched down behind a log and scanned the place. The other building, square in shape, sat about fifty yards next to it. Behind both of them, I noticed a small, shed-looking building and another smaller building. I thought I saw a partial rooftop of a barn way on the other side, but I couldn't be certain.

The real question was: where did they have her? And were they watching me right now? For a moment, I looked into the trees around me, searching for cameras. I saw nothing but snow and a handful of birds. A cardinal seemed to be staring at me. Then, just like that, he fluttered away, sailing in the direction of the buildings.

I was envious of both his speed and his elusiveness. I briefly recalled dreams of flying when I was a kid. Who didn't, right? Well, I'd actually had the same types of dreams—flying through the air like one of Robin Hood's arrows—when I first got married to Nicole. Never told anyone. People would think I was crazy.

Like now. I wondered if my brain was beginning to freeze over. I began moving again, making my way down the rocky terrain, looking for spots behind a tree or large boulder to pause and look for any sign of human life. Four separate times, I stopped. Each time I saw nothing. On the last stop, I was close enough to see the windows of the L-shaped building. Some were covered. For the ones that weren't, I saw no movement, nothing inside, although the day's glare didn't help.

As an owl hooted above me in a tree somewhere, I scooted to the edge of the first building—the square one with two stories. Part of me wondered if I should simply shout out: "I'm here, I'm here." Would a man walk outside with Mackenzie at his side?

My mind went back to the uncertainty of this entire pursuit. Not knowing who had her and, just as importantly, not knowing why or what they wanted was eating a hole in my stomach. Literally. I'd never had an ulcer, but right now it felt like acid was leaking into my body cavity.

I edged around the building, shooting quick glances at the uncovered windows. A few pieces of furniture, but it looked uninhabited. She could be on the second floor. Onward. Around the next corner, I found a large metal door. I pulled on the handle. It didn't budge. I cupped my hands against the thin vertical window. I saw a long hallway with a few chairs tossed on their sides.

I futilely tugged on the door handle a few more times. It rattled but didn't budge. I had two options. Find a big rock and bust out a first-floor window, crawl inside, and inspect the second floor. Or just move on to the L-shaped building. I chose the path of less noise.

Just then, I heard what sounded like the whine of an engine. I put a hand to my ear. Was that an actual noise or my hearing aid screwing with me? I raced in the direction of where I thought the noise had come from. I ran as fast as my numb legs would move, the woods that sloped up the hillside on my left, the L-shaped building to the right. I felt like a four-legged animal on two legs. Maybe a gorilla.

My eyes darted all around me, searching for any movement, human or otherwise. Even glanced in the windows I ran by. Nothing.

Another sound. An engine revving? Again, though, I trusted my hearing like a man might trust his cheating wife. Never.

Finally, I reached the end of the L-shaped building. My eyes went straight to the far edge of the deeper woods. The back end of a silver Jeep was slogging through mounds of snow and mud.

My heart sunk. Was Mackenzie in that car?

The Jeep disappeared around a bend.

Twenty-Eight

They were gone. No way I could catch them on foot. I put my hands on my knees and panted. My entire insides burned—my lungs from running so hard and my stomach from feeling like a knife had a ripped a hole in it.

With my pulse still peppering the side of my neck, I pushed to a standing position. The first thing that caught my eye was a barn, or what was left of it. The front doors were, essentially, shrapnel. The roof was all but gone.

I flipped around and stared at the L-shaped building. Could the driver of the Jeep have left Mackenzie here at the compound? Or was this some kind of setup?

"Think, dammit. Think." My voice sounded like Elmer Fudd. My lips were foreign objects.

Maybe they had been watching me all along. But for how long? Once I stepped on the property? Before then? I tried to think about my drive up from Elkins. I'd passed a few cars. A couple were behind me, but nothing had stood out. I didn't recall a Jeep. It could have been there, though.

Professionals could be involved. The thought of "professionals" made me think about the *yakuza* again. It was impossible to understand who was here or even why, at this point.

I'd left my phone in my car—nice move, Oz—but unless I called Sheriff Kupchak, and that was not really an option, a phone would get me nowhere.

One option. Search the L-shaped building and then move on to the smaller buildings, as long as there was an unlocked door. If I found nothing, then I'd hike back to the road, try to flag down a truck, or, better yet, just call for a tow. Once back in town, Denise would probably kick my ass.

I trudged over to the first door I came to in the L-shaped building and yanked. It opened. Once inside, I found the temperature maybe only five or ten degrees warmer. But that was still five or ten degrees warmer. I blew into my hands, and after walking no more than twenty feet, I saw two enormous doors, both open, to my left. I quickly moved to the threshold.

"Ho-ly shit." I was staring at a sanctuary. It looked like a bomb had exploded in it, but I saw pipes from an organ, pews turned on their sides. I leaned over and picked up a red book and thumbed through a few tattered pages. It was a hymnal. At the far end, four steps led to a lectern, also on its side. There was a closed door off to the left. I jogged in that direction—my legs had begun to thaw some. I weaved around the mess, made it to the door, and pushed it open. I found two offices. More furniture, but the filing cabinets were bare naked. Made sense if the Feds had raided the place.

For a split second, my thoughts went back a week to the raid at Novak and Novak. The first domino to my life turning upside down, or so it seemed. And that raid, which had led to Dad's first heart attack, was nothing like this raid, from what Brook had described.

I marched back through the sanctuary and out the double doors, heading down a hallway lined with rooms. I stopped and searched each one. After about ten rooms, it began to feel redundant. As if I were wasting my time. As if I were being played a fool. But I was here. And I'd seen a Jeep. This wasn't a suburban mall where cars came and went nonstop. That vehicle had been here for a purpose.

Was that purpose to do nothing more than screw with my mind? If so, it was beginning to work. I took another thirty minutes to finish the search of the floor. Not a sign of any person—no articles of clothing or even candy wrappers.

I ambled up to the second floor and immediately felt a breeze. I looked down the hall. Something moved. I snapped my hand around to my back and grabbed the pistol. I leaned against the wall, dropped lower, and inched forward.

There it was again.

Something fluttered. I squinted. Was that a dress? Maybe some type of curtain? Part of me begged to call out Mackenzie's name. It was all I could do to keep the sense of dread at bay.

I shuffled forward another twenty feet, then stopped cold. A piece of tattered plastic was fluttering into the hallway. There had to be an open window in the room. Was that it, though?

I kept moving, my gun at my side. I told myself not to pull the trigger at the first sign of human life—it could be Mackenzie.

Almost at the door, I paused, put my hand against the wall. I felt no movement and heard only plastic fluttering. Without wasting another moment, I wheeled around the opening and peered inside. Sheets of plastic hung from an exposed ceiling. Most of the far wall, as best as I could tell, wasn't there. I could see trees, even some snow.

A few steps in, I felt the intensity of the wind. The plastic hung like shower curtains, ones that were stained and had tears in them. I edged forward, then stopped. I could see something up ahead between the flapping plastic. It was gray and black, maybe three feet off the floor. I did a quick three-sixty to make sure no one was sneaking up on me. All clear.

I gripped the gun with one hand, shoved plastic aside with my opposite forearm. It was coming into focus. It looked like a chair. I shuffled a few more feet, my head still scanning all around me. As I weaved around each sheet of plastic, the gaping hole in the wall became more obvious. Looked like a window had caved in, as well as the support beams just around it. A quick glance above my head. Parts of the ceiling were missing. I saw pipes and exposed wires, some dangling, shaking in the wind. The whole structure seemed unstable, as if it had been built by amateurs. An HGTV remodel wouldn't do the trick. This place was destined for a demolition. I just hoped the house of cards would say upright while I was still...

Wait. Was that an arm?

I plowed through plastic, moving so fast I got tangled in one sheet. I flailed my arms. The gun went off. I choked on my own spit as dust and debris rained down on me.

"Fucking gun!" I put the safety on and shoved the pistol back into my waistband.

But then I realized something. When the gun had fired, no one cried out; no one moved. *Maybe because there was no one?*

I spun from the hold of the plastic sheet and smacked the other sheets to the side, making a beeline toward the arm that I thought I'd seen. I got past the last sheet, and I saw a person behind a chair.

"Denise!" I ran over, dropped to her side. Her eyes were open, staring at nothing. I shook her. Her head rocked left and right, almost as if it wasn't attached to her body. I spotted a needle next to my knee. Her shirt sleeve was pushed up above her elbow. Needle holes showed in the crook of her arm. I put my hand on her wrist.

No pulse. I touched her face. Cold, clammy.

She was dead. Fucking dead.

And I was to blame

Twenty-Nine

I touched her face again. "Who the hell did this to you? Why? Why, why, why?" I screamed at the top of my lungs. Tears welled, but they were snuffed out by an anger so deep I could feel my whole body quake.

"Fuck!" I slammed my fist to the floor. I did it again and again and again. I did it until the skin on the side of my hand cracked open from the lip of cracked linoleum. Blood smeared across my hand. I wiped it on my jeans as another round of tears filled my eyes. I stared at Denise, wondering how she had gotten here, and why. I couldn't think. I grunted out a breath, then another, trying to keep it together.

I got to my feet, shuffled closer to the gaping hole in the wall, and looked across the property toward the thicker area of woods. I could see the path the Jeep had taken, but I saw no sign of the vehicle itself. Dammit, if only I could have read the license plate number. I'd been too slow.

I flipped on my heels and stared at Denise. Had the *yakuza* lured us to this town and finally killed her? If not them, then who was behind it? Was it even the same group of people who had kidnapped Mackenzie in Hawaii? And with me leaving Denise alone, had that given them the opportunity they needed to grab her?

I pinched the corner of my eyes. Bile seeped into the back of my throat. This wasn't happening. This had to be a nightmare.

I opened my eyes, took in a few breaths. My eyes went to the chair in front of Denise. A video camera was sitting on it. I walked around Denise, picked up the camera. The viewer on the side was flipped open. I found the metal *ON* button and pushed it. The tiny screen on the side came to life. I tapped the arrow to play the video.

It was Denise, sitting on the floor here in this room. She was crying, wailing even. A man held her from behind, gripping the back of her neck. Hard. I couldn't see his face. It was off screen. Probably on purpose.

Lots of yelling and crying. A man telling her something. I found the volume button and cranked it louder. "Just do it. Do it if you want your kid to stay alive," he said. His accent was similar to the other West Virginia locals I'd spoken to.

She looked up at the camera, tears streaming down her face. Then she picked up a rubber band, tied it around her upper arm.

"Dear God," I said. "No, Denise. Tell me they didn't make you—" I stopped short, my eyes wet but glued to the tiny screen.

The man who was holding her from behind handed her a needle. She took it from him and just stared at it, her eyes wide with fear. She had to be thinking about her life ending, and the one she'd never see again. Mackenzie.

I swallowed a lump in my throat. I wondered how long her stare-down would continue. A few seconds later, I got my answer. The man smacked the side of her head. I flinched.

"Denise," I said, touching the screen, wishing, praying there was a way to go back in time, to stop this from happening.

I heard a chuckle. Maybe by the person holding the camera? Hard to tell, but it made my stomach churn.

With her hair draped across her face, she slowly pushed herself upward. Then, without warning, she swung her arm to the side— the one holding the needle. She was trying to stab the man who held her. His legs hopped back. She missed, lost her balance, and dropped to the side.

The camera began to shake…the person holding it was moving, but never did the video show any faces other than Denise's. The man behind Denise grabbed her by the hair, pulled her upright. Expletives by more than one voice. I couldn't understand everything. Then the man pointed at the camera and said, "Do it. You've got to do it, Denise, or we kill Mackenzie. Do you hear me?"

I hit pause. I could barely breathe; I was gasping for air. I wasn't sure I could watch much more. I turned away, looked at Denise on the floor. I had to watch the video until the end. They wanted me to see it. Maybe there would be additional information about Mackenzie at the end.

My mind went straight to the worst-case scenario: what if these hicks who killed Denise didn't have Mackenzie? They could know about it, somehow, through some connection in Hawaii.

"Fuck!" I yelled, stomping my foot. I pushed the play button.

A moment later, I saw the barrel of a gun. The man pressed it to the side of her head. She got still, although her eyes darted around like that of a bird. More tears, her mouth stuck open, as if she were releasing a silent scream. I'd never seen anyone so terrorized.

It felt like I'd been stabbed in the gut, and someone was just cranking it around and around.

Back to the video.

"Come on, Denise. We don't have all day. Do it. You know you want it anyway. You're nothing but a two-bit crack whore. You've always wanted to end your life. This is easy. We're giving you the opportunity to do it for Mackenzie. If you don't, we'll be forced to kill her. We don't want to, but let's face it. You're not going to live much longer. You might as well go out on a high."

Both men chuckled at the sick humor. The camera bounced up and down so much I thought I got a quick glimpse of the man's face behind Denise. Maybe just a chin.

The video continued as Denise put her hands over her face and sobbed. A few seconds passed. She finally pulled her hands down. Her face was bloated, red, quivering.

"Denise?" the man warned, pressing the gun harder against her head.

She looked into the camera now. "I'm sorry, Mackenzie. Mommy will always love you."

And then she took the needle and pressed it into her arm.

I wanted to throw the camera down, smash it into a million pieces. But there were still a few more seconds. It didn't take long. She became wobbly, her eyes got heavy, and then she dropped to an elbow. She licked her lips, as if her mouth had been drained of all liquid. Her body collapsed to the floor. Her eyes appeared to flicker for a moment, and then they ceased movement.

The camera moved again, down to the boots of the man holding it. Words were spoken, but they were indiscernible. And then the video stopped.

A three-ton weight was caving in my chest. With my eyes looking at Denise, I raised the camera above my head. I was broken, but more than that, I was angry. At myself for not bringing her with me, or maybe for not forcing her to stay back in Hawaii. Angry at the heathens who did this to her. Wind whipped across the space, but I was sweating. My eyes were on fire.

A second before I slammed the camera to the ground, I held up. Somehow, a thread of rational thought made it to my frontal lobe. This could be evidence to find the assholes who'd killed Denise. I needed to keep it. I looked at the video camera, a newer model. I rotated it in my hands, unsure where the data was stored. Hidden next to the battery compartment was a tiny button, which

I pushed, and out slipped a little memory card. I placed it into my pocket.

Damn, I wished I had my phone. I had no clue where Mackenzie could be. My best hope was getting this video snippet to some type of expert who could break it down, look for clues as to who these men were. Their voices, clothes, the gun, along with who drove a Jeep.

I had to go to the authorities. For help in finding out who'd killed Denise, who held Mackenzie and where. Still, I felt more lost than ever. They'd said not to bring the police in. Damn, this whole riddle bullshit now seemed like a twisted prank. I still couldn't envision the end-game. Did the people who'd killed Denise have Mackenzie? Was she being held in some cabin nearby? Or was she a world away, having been sold to some Asian child trafficker?

I bent down next to Denise and gently pressed her eyes shut. I closed my eyes and said a few words. I wasn't sure how to pray, what to say. All I could think of was saying how sorry I was and how I hoped she was in a place of peace.

I thought about hiking back to the main road, to figure out my next steps. But I knew I couldn't leave her here. I put an arm under her legs and one under her back and hoisted her up. Carrying her through this terrain wouldn't be easy. In fact, it would push me to the limit. Whatever. She was my daughter's mother. She'd been forced to overdose on some type of drug. I owed it to her. I had to do this.

As I started walking around the plastic sheets toward the door, I used my knee to push her up a bit, get a better grip. I felt something crinkle against my fingertips. I moved them around and felt a piece of paper. I walked across the hall into another room. No open windows or holes in the wall. There was an old sheet in the corner. I gently laid her on the floor, then turned her on her side.

A note was taped to her lower back. I pulled it off and read it:

Do not be diverted by the death of someone who does not matter. Her life would have ended soon enough anyway. She was flawed. So far you have passed the test. For that, we are pleased. If you want to see Mackenzie you will follow the trail: where the Prophet was first swaddled, the birth of a nation first formed, and the Old Sandwich reaches the State.

One additional detail. You have 6 hours to accomplish this goal. If you do not reach the destination within this time, or if you contact authorities, we will be forced to kill her.

Good luck.

Six hours. *The death of someone who does not matter.* I glanced at Denise and felt a volcanic surge of emotion. Had she been used as nothing more than a pawn?

Six hours. I blinked a couple of times, my mind scrambled with questions, trying to somehow comprehend how all this could be, who these people were, what kind of fucked-up game was being played out.

Six hours. *So far you have passed the test.* Could it be…that Mackenzie's kidnapping, the assault, Gwen's murder, this cross-country search was more about *me*? Me. Why me?

Six hours. I stared at the note, focusing on the riddle part again: *where the Prophet was first swaddled, the birth of a nation first formed, and the Old Sandwich reaches the State.*

Prophet. Birth of a nation. Old Sandwich? It made no sense. My brain was either fried or frozen, or just simply in shock. It wasn't operating at full capacity. Maybe not even at fifty percent.

Six hours. Mackenzie wasn't close, but she wasn't terribly far, this note told me. Not in another country, anyway. I had to get out of here, to find transportation, to get some help in figuring out this riddle. No authorities, just like last time. I'd have to keep it under wraps.

I jumped to my feet, grabbed a sheet from the corner, and laid it over Denise. God, I hated leaving her here. But she would want me to go after Mackenzie.

Six hours.

I raced out of the building still with a trace of hope that within a matter of hours, somehow, some way, I'd be able to finally hold my daughter in my arms.

Thirty

The door to Joseph's hut opened, and Cecelia walked in, interrupting his moment of peace.

"Please tell me you have a good reason for doing this." His voice was monotone as he stared at a cross on the wall, his heart beating at fifty-four beats a minute.

She held out a hand. "We've received the call. Here."

Without looking at her, he took the phone and brought it to his ear. "Good news, Charlie?"

"It happened just like you said it would, Joseph. He arrived right after we left. We watched him from the forest."

Charlie's voice sounded like a kid who'd just ridden a roller coaster. "Calm down, Charlie. Let's not get too excited. But this does indeed sound like good news." He could feel Cecelia's eyes on him, but he chose to continue studying the cross. "Charlie, are you sure he didn't see you or Tovar, or that Jeep of yours?"

"Uh, no sir. No way. We were long gone."

"Very nice."

"It was just so surreal, sir. You said he'd leave her behind. He did. You said he'd figure out a way into Camp Israel. He did. You said he'd grieve over her loss. We were able to see him through my high-powered lens as he discovered her body. We saw him staring into the camera viewer. He was clearly devastated. Just like you said."

Joseph nodded. "Are you saying you had doubted me?"

A pause.

"No, no sir. It's just, uh, great that it all happened according to plan, that's all."

"Very nice work, Charlie. How does it feel to contribute to the cause of the Kingdom?"

"Me and Tovar, we're just so excited. I mean, killing that girl. Well, of course, she actually killed herself. You were right. It felt...I don't know, exhilarating."

Joseph could hear the pair giggling like school children.

"Now, Charlie, we don't need to celebrate the death of another human being. Even if she was a sinner and will surely end up in hell. We cannot mock those who refuse to feel the blessings of the Lord."

"True, Joseph. Thank you for the reminder."

"You left the note?"

"Just as you said, yes."

"Very well. So, on we march to the next phase."

"Sir?"

"Yes, Charlie?"

"Me and Tovar...well, we were wondering if there is some way we could contribute to this phase. We know we'd have to boogie over to—"

"Charlie, I appreciate your desire to contribute, to be one of the leaders of this effort. But we all have a role to play in His world. Me, you, Cecelia. Everyone. You have played your role. Others will prepare to execute their tasks. And soon, oh so very soon, Charlie, it will all come to fruition. When it does, we will all celebrate. And that celebration will spread, soon covering this earth like a giant tidal wave. People will see the will of Him, and they will follow and open their hearts, just like you and the others in the Kingdom."

Charlie sang his praises for another two minutes as Joseph opened a magazine and thumbed a few pages. Finally, he grew tired of the lavish compliments and ended the call. He lifted to his feet, put on a coat.

"Where are you going?"

He didn't respond to Cecelia. He knew she would follow, just like the others. He left the hut and circled to the back. The sun was peeking through the clouds. There was a chill in the air, but there were only patches of white from the snowstorm a week earlier. A few of the other members who were working on chores bowed their heads when he passed. Joseph walked into the woods, Cecelia close on his heels. They knew they would not be followed—Kingdom members knew this was Holy soil and required special permission to enter.

They walked another two hundred yards, crossed a creek, and then trekked up the bank of a small hill. They stopped where two boulders marked the spot.

"Move the leaves," he said.

"Why do you want to do this?" she asked.

He shifted his eyes to her. She quickly looked away and did as he commanded. Under the leaves was a fatigue-green tarp. She pulled it back, unveiling a hole that was ten feet by six feet. He gazed upon the stack of bodies. For some reason, he enjoyed counting them. One, two, three, four, five, six. Young men, young women, even one child. Sacrifices, he knew, were an inevitable step in the process of redemption. Of finding the one whose blood carried the essence of Him.

He felt a tingle pass through his arms as he considered the mass grave.

A moment passed, and then he heard a sniffle. He looked at Cecelia, who was staring into the hole, wiping a tear from her cheek.

"Why are you sad?"

"Seeing people die...it just seems unnecessary." Her voice was weak, as though she questioned whether she should have spoken those words. But he was glad she'd shared her thoughts. Now he knew her position.

"When you joined me on this journey, Cecelia, we knew that as mere mortals we could not lead our flock. I did not choose this path," he said, holding a finger in the air. "It was chosen for me."

She looked into his eyes. For a moment, he saw the impressionable young girl he'd met when she'd worked as a guide in one of the many museums in DC. Her unassuming nature had hidden a beautiful young woman. Her features were soft, her skin buttery smooth. It wasn't long thereafter that he could sense her need for divine guidance. To hold a real purpose in life.

He knew, at some level, everyone had that need. But for many, it would be almost impossible to unearth. It was buried under so much false pretense. So many people in the world were self-absorbed. Not just the obvious ones, the loathsome hedge-fund managers, the politicians, the slimy salespeople. No, the ones who really boggled his mind were the ones who pretended they were all about making the world a better place: the doctors who cared only about making history, not about curing the sick; the lawyers who cared only about winning, not finding the path to innocence and salvation. Nurses, preachers, teachers...on and on and on.

Every facet of society was devoured in this endless race to accumulate stuff, to show off their trophies of success. They knew nothing of how to sacrifice for each other with humility, without shouting their self-righteous success to the world. But Joseph had become enlightened. He had looked inward and felt something touch his heart. Something that he couldn't deny or turn away from. He went through a period of self-reflection on a level that very few could claim. Through his evolution, a vision came to him. It was clear, peaceful, at least at its core. Through divine guidance, he'd been chosen to carry the torch, to develop a flock of followers who would carry out the will of Him. But Joseph knew he was not without flaws. To be the leader of the flock, the one who the world would eventually see as the spiritual trailblazer, it required a sacrifice of the person who carried the blood of Him.

He closed his eyes for a moment, thinking, *"Let it be written, let it be done."*

"Seven is a very biblical number," he said to Cecelia, whose eyes were once again on the bodies in the grave. "This was fate, my dear, that it took seven times to find the right one."

She pressed her lips together and gave a single nod. "He still hasn't made it all the way yet."

"You are so very right, Cecelia. While it is close, we cannot completely predict human behavior." He gently touched her arm.

She looked at his hand, then put her hand over his. "I'm sorry if it seemed like I was doubting you, our purpose. I understand that to rid the world of hate and greed, to wake people up to follow our path of enlightenment, the path is not always easy or smooth."

He smiled, and she moved closer. "You make me proud, Cecelia. You have grown so much since I first met you." He brushed the side of her cheek. "You are beautiful from the inside out. And if I see it through my eyes and my heart, then God sees it. We will reach our goal. I feel it." He put a fist against his chest. "And once we do, the rest will follow."

Hand in hand, they walked back to the camp, and his mind momentarily pictured life after the sacrifice. His spirit would be whole. He would break down barriers, bring people together, and lead this growing Kingdom.

He'd been chosen. He was ready.

Thirty-One

By the time I reached the main road, my lungs were on fire. Which, in and of itself was a strange sensation, because the rest of my body felt like it had been frozen in a glacier for the last eighty years.

Hands on my knees for a few deep breaths. The video of Denise played in my head, the beating she took, her unwillingness to take her own life and then realizing there was no way out—the plunge of the needle into her arm. I wanted to vomit. But more than that, I wanted to find these fuckers who'd killed her and do the same to them. Even worse. And I wanted to find Mackenzie. I had to find Mackenzie. Denise wouldn't want me to spend time mourning her death—that much I knew with certainty.

I trudged over to my car, crawled in through the open window, and grabbed my phone. I knew my car was useless until I found someone to pull me out of the snowbank. I only had six hours, though. Actually less than six hours. That trek back to the road had taken forty minutes. I stared at my phone for a second, wondering who to call first.

The latest riddle flashed across my mind again—it was on a continuous loop in my brain.

If you want to see Mackenzie you will follow the trail: where the Prophet was first swaddled, the birth of a nation first formed, and the Old Sandwich reaches the State.

Prophet. Jesus? My parents were Jewish by birth, me by adoption, but none of us really practiced Judaism. I was raised to believe Jesus was a prophet. In reality, I had no clue or any urge to pick apart religious minutiae. I only wanted the answer to this part of the riddle. Maybe the writers of this riddle were referencing another religion. Or, it could be Moses or one of Jesus's disciples, Mathew, Mark, Luke, or John.

The third part of the riddle, speaking of an Old Sandwich reaching the State, made absolutely no sense. The middle piece—the birth of a nation first formed—seemed more straightforward. I assumed it was talking about the United States. If that was the case, the location had to be on the East Coast somewhere. I could think of a handful of cities—Philadelphia, DC, Boston. Or, depending on how they looked at history, one of the early American settlements. Jamestown, Virginia, came to mind. Other than that, I'd need to check other sources for the information. Or get some damn help.

I looked up and saw a car rounding the bend on the main road, headed my way. I practically fell out of the car, dropping into a pile of snow. I crawled to the road and stood up, waving my arms.

As it moved closer, I could see it was a blue pickup, a Ford, at least ten years old. Something was sticking up from the bed of the pickup, but I couldn't make it out.

The vehicle started to veer across the yellow line in the middle of the road. Dammit, he was trying to go around me.

"Hold up! I need your help!" I jumped up and down and pointed at my car. "Stop!"

The driver either didn't see me or he did and was trying to avoid me. The pickup was now completely in the opposite lane. I shuffled over to the other lane.

Nice move, Oz. You want to play a game of chicken with a two-ton object moving at sixty miles per hour? That's not something you'll win. And if you lose, then Mackenzie loses.

The pickup still didn't slow down. In fact, it moved back to the original lane. And so did I. The pickup was now a hundred yards and closing fast. Rational thoughts were not making their way to my frontal lobe. In my mind, I had only one choice to not delay this any further. I reached behind my back, pulled my gun out, and aimed it right at the windshield.

The pickup slammed on its brakes, launching a chair from the bed right at me. I dove into the snow as the chair crashed to the pavement. Somehow it didn't shatter into a hundred pieces. Whatever. I scrambled to my feet and ran to the driver's-side window. An older man was practically hugging the steering wheel, his sunken eyes unblinking. Raccoon eyes.

"Roll down the window," I said.

He didn't move. He looked scared but also defiant. I realized I was waving the gun around like it was an extension of my hand. I was starting to rethink my decision.

"Can you please roll down the window? I need help." I flipped around and pointed at the car stuck in the snow. When I turned back around, I saw his hand slowly making its way toward the console.

"Put your hands where I can see them," I said quickly, instantly realizing how cliché that sounded. I raised my gun again and aimed it through the window. The man's arms went up so fast he banged his hands off the roof.

"I'm not here to hurt you. I just need your help."

His eyes were frozen on me.

"Did you hear me?"

A single nod.

"Again, I don't want to hurt you. I won't hurt you." I paused, looking for an acknowledgement. Nothing. I wondered if he was literally experiencing some type of shock or nervous breakdown.

I glanced up and down the road. No sign of more cars. I looked to the man. "Please, sir, I really need your help. I'm desperate. Someone has kidnapped my daughter, and I have no way—"

Before I finished, the window slid down. "Why didn't you say that to begin with?" His voice matched his appearance, that of an old codger.

"I'm sorry for pulling the gun. Really, I am." I looked at his console. "You don't have a gun in here, do you?"

"Would that make a difference?"

He was still testing me. "I just don't want you to shoot me. I'm going to put my gun in my waistband, okay?" I did what I said, then rested my hands on the car, where he could see them. "Do you have a chain or rope in your truck? I need someone to pull my car out of the snowbank."

"Nope. Sorry. As you can see, my truck is full of furniture."

I glanced at the pickup bed and saw chairs, tables, a few boxes. They didn't seem to be very organized. Then again, that might have happened when he'd skidded to a stop. Thanks to me.

"One of my chairs is now in the middle of the road, thanks to you," he said.

Thanks all around. "Okay, no chain. Uh…" I looked to my right, trying to think what I should do next. Staying in this exact spot seemed like it would only waste more time. My eyes went to the chair in the road. I ran over and picked it up. One of legs was broken, hanging on by a few splinters. I brought it back to the truck. "Sorry."

"You've said that enough. Throw it in the back, then get in the truck."

I was in the passenger seat in seconds, looking right at him. "What's your name?"

"Virgil, and I'm headed into town. You can fill me in while I drive. Better put your seat belt on. My wife says I drive like a bat out of hell."

Thirty-Two

Virgil's wife knew what she was talking about. We hadn't traveled more than a mile when Virgil hit a patch of black ice and the pickup fishtailed. For a brief moment, I thought we were headed straight for a tree at more than fifty miles per hour. Somehow, he kept the truck on the road.

"Damn, that almost gave me a heart attack," I said, a hand to my chest.

"The Beast survives all." He patted the dash and cracked a smile. I saw more gaps than teeth. He waited a beat, then said, "Nice coat."

I looked down at my yellow raincoat and back up at him. He was still grinning. I said, "Uh, yeah. Very funny." I decided to take advantage of the lighthearted moment, if you could call it that. "Say, what do you know about what went on at Camp Israel?"

"I know a few whackos held a bunch of people in the compound. They treated women like slaves, raped them, beat them. I believed they even killed kids." He shook his head. "Just sick, that's how it made me and Ida feel. And for what? Religion? I'm tired of hearing about how religious conviction was some kind of justification for hurting, even killing another person. I don't give two shits what religion they're talking about, either."

I wanted to give Virgil a fist bump, but I doubted he knew what one was, and I didn't want him thinking I was being aggressive toward him. I also needed fresh information; what he'd told me was basically what I already knew. Of course, that was what I'd asked him—to tell me about what had gone on at Camp Israel. And he'd answered the question straight up and with passion. But I wasn't sure exactly what to ask him. Hell, he could be one of them. I let it go for the moment.

"Is there a car-rental place in town?" I almost cringed when I asked, knowing the answer.

He chuckled. "You're joking, right? We have one motel. One church. One donut shop. Well, there used to be a couple of others, until Fred started acting like he was some hifalutin real-estate mogul."

The donut-shop wars. I wasn't going there.

"So, no place to rent a car. Maybe I could buy a cheap used one."

"Hmm," was all he said. He draped a wrist over the steering wheel, his gaze looking out across the road and wilderness. I assumed he was thinking of places to help me find a car.

I decided to take a chance that this guy was okay. "Hey, while you're in deep thought, I need to make a call."

He moaned something and nodded.

I punched up Brook's number. As it started to ring, I added, "Okay, so, I'm calling a friend of mine in law enforcement. Some of this stuff you're going to hear might blow your mind. But it's real, and if I don't figure this out, someone is going to kill my daughter."

"Well, quit wasting time. Hell, get on with it."

I nodded, the phone pressed to my ear.

"Ozzie…hey." It was Brook, and she sounded out of breath.

"Something wrong?" I asked.

"No, just had to run to get to my phone. Just got out of my shower." I checked the time on my phone. It was just after six o'clock in the Eastern time zone.

"Shower?"

"Yeah, long story. Been working long shifts on this stakeout. Doesn't matter. What's going on?"

"They killed Denise, Brook. They fucking killed her." I glanced at Virgil, who didn't change his expression—just kept looking straight ahead.

"What? Dear God, Ozzie, are you okay?"

"I'm fine." I gave her a twenty-second summary of Denise's murder, how I found her and the video. Then I told her about the note and the second riddle.

"Tell me the riddle again. It's not really clicking. Wait, can you take a quick picture and send it to me?"

"Good idea." I pulled the note from my pocket, snapped a shot, and sent it off.

I took another look at Virgil, who was now tugging on flaps of skin around his neck. He had a few to spare. But he was still stoic.

"Got it yet?" I asked Brook.

"Just came in."

I could hear mumbling, but that was about it. I gave her a good thirty seconds before I jumped back in. "Look, unless you're some type of psychic, this riddle seems—"

"Impossible," she said. "I'm reading this to myself, and I don't know what the hell they're trying to convey. Apparently, it's some type of location. Hold on a second. On this middle one, the birth of a nation...I'm wondering if they could be referring to Williamsburg, Virginia."

"That's one I hadn't thought about."

"Went there on vacation as a kid. It's part of what they call the Historical Triangle, along with Jamestown and Yorktown."

"I guess I slept through that part of history. Anyway, while that's good information, it makes me queasy. The number of possibilities just went up. And I think, ultimately, that's the easiest part of the riddle to solve."

"It'll be okay. We just need to think this through."

"Did you read the note? I've only got six hours." Damn, I sounded like an ass. "Sorry. I'm just…"

"I get it, Oz. I'm a big girl. Now's not the time to worry about that crap, anyway. We have to be efficient in how we work to solve this riddle, get you to this location—gotta believe it's somewhere on the East Coast—and hope and pray you can get Mackenzie. Now, for starters, I want us to be in sync with how much time we've got."

"Right. Makes sense." Another picture of Denise being whacked across the head popped into my mind.

"So, do you know the exact time you found Denise and the note?"

I exhaled, then looked at my phone. "I'm guessing it was around 5:20 local time."

"Hold on. How would they know when that six-hour timer started?"

She had a point. I hadn't even taken a moment to think that through, my mind was in such chaos. "Not sure."

"It's either a hoax—"

"You know I can't believe that right now."

"I was going to say that they could just be giving an estimated time."

That reminded me of the Jeep. I filled her in on that arm of the story.

"You see, right there, they could be using that as their approximate time. Or they could have had eyes on you."

"No one else was there. At least I don't think anyone was there."

"I mean a camera, Oz. They were watching you."

A cold chill went up my spine. It made sense. "Okay, I'm following you. Still, I'm guessing 5:20."

"So, we have until 11:20 tonight, Eastern time."

That left us with five hours and fifteen minutes. "Brook, I want to say this is possible, but right now, I don't know how." I could feel a quake in my chest. "I'm stuck in bumfuck West Virginia. I've got no wheels, no idea where I'm going, what or who I'm up against. And each passing minute feels like I'm losing an hour."

Virgil waved a hand in front of my face. I noticed we'd just made it into town. He started pointing off to the left.

"You're not in this alone, Oz," Brook said.

"Want to bet? They did this for me. You saw the note. This whole game was about setting up some type of test for me. Why? I have no clue. None. And that's why I'm so fucking pissed right now!"

Virgil was flapping his hand now.

"What?" I asked, turning to him for a second.

"I've got the solution to your car problem."

"Did I just hear that correctly?" Brook asked.

"I think so."

Virgil pulled onto a snow-sprinkled gravel driveway that ran along the side of a house. "Well, you deal with that and get on the road," she said.

A bit of hope refreshed my brain. "Listen, Brook, I know I've said we can't afford to bring in anyone else to help find Mackenzie. But I'm not sure we have that luxury any more. I think we're going to have to take that chance."

"I was going to do it anyway."

"Thanks…I think."

"You know the saying: it's easier to ask forgiveness than to beg permission."

I told her I'd call her when I was headed east. As I ended the call, I slipped out of the pickup and saw Virgil throwing the furniture from the back of the pickup into the front yard of the house.

"What are you doing?"

"It's my son's furniture. He's in there playing video games. He can get his lazy ass off the couch and come out and get it."

"Do you need any help?" I was still waiting to hear his solution for my car issue.

He didn't respond, so I jumped up into the bed and helped him unload a couch, a dresser, and three boxes. "Give me a minute," he said before disappearing inside the house.

Just thirty seconds later, he was walking back out, a large coat in his hands. He tossed it at me. It was one of those North Face coats.

"Put that on. It's Junior's, but he doesn't have any sense to wear the damn thing. It'll keep you warm just in case the Beast gives you a problem."

"Do what?"

He extended his arm, dangling a key chain in front of my face. "Come on now. You've got to get on the road. I heard you. You need to get to somewhere on the East Coast."

"But that's your car, Virgil."

He took two paces and grabbed hold of my arms. "You have a missing daughter. There's apparently already been one death. Her mother, I'm guessing. Don't question this. I thought my daughter had been kidnapped years ago. Turns out she was just at a friend's house. But for a few hours, I thought my insides were going to disintegrate."

I grabbed the keys from his hand as a surge of emotion creeped into the back of my throat. "I'm not sure what to say except 'thank you.' Thank you so much. How can I get the truck back to you?"

"Worry about that later, once you get Mackenzie back. You get her back, I'll be the second happiest guy in the world. Now go on and get out of here."

He pulled me closer and thumped my back twice.

Wearing my new coat, I blew out of Elkins, almost daring Sheriff Kupchak to pull me over.

Thirty-Three

———◦◦◦———

By the time I passed Peggy's Diner on Highway 33, I'd already spoken to Brook twice. The first call was to confirm my general direction. We agreed I should head straight for DC. If later we decided I should veer south toward Virginia, I wouldn't lose that much time. If, however, the answer to all of this riddle crap was in Philadelphia, or even worse, Boston, then a miracle would be required to get me there on time.

I tried not to think in terms of miracles. Counting on miracles was counting on something I couldn't control. As it was, I was dictating essentially nothing in this process.

The second call from Brook was to notify me that I would be receiving another call shortly. It would be on a secure line—as secure as one could be, considering I was on an open cell. "Secure line" meant the FBI was involved. The conference call would include Brook, Stan, and Nick. It gave me a needed boost that I wasn't in this alone, but uneasiness came with it. "These people have been one step ahead of me this entire time. Like they predicted this whole scenario. Do they not know, Brook, that you're friends with Stan, whose cousin works for the FBI?"

"If they do know, I'm sure you would have heard about it by now. On top of that, I've been informed that the FBI's involvement is off the books. For now, just Nick. If it expands beyond that, you'll know about it. If you're not comfortable with it, then we won't make the move."

I had to admit, she was right. We'd ended the call, and I continued my trek to DC, going as much over sixty as the Beast would allow without slipping on the snowy roads. Every half mile or so, I'd feel the back end swing around—a signal that I'd run the pickup across a patch of black ice—and I'd literally break out into a sweat until all four tires were firmly gripping the road.

The line rang, and I punched up the call and put it on speaker. Stan did the quick introduction to his cousin, Nick. They sounded so similar—some type of Brooklyn accents—it was difficult to distinguish their voices. At least it was for me.

"You're headed for DC, correct?" Nick asked, not wasting time with pleasantries.

"Yes," I said. "I should be there in three hours and fifteen minutes. Brook, how much time do I have left in my six-hour window?"

"Just under five hours."

"How much under?" I asked.

"By thirty seconds."

"I don't mean to nitpick you, but—"

"I know, every second counts, Oz."

"All right," Nick said. "Brook sent us the picture of the note. I've read it over a couple of times. Before I offer an opinion—Stan or Brook, you got anything?"

"I'm thinking Philadelphia," Stan said. "The First Continental Congress met there; they wrote the Declaration of Independence there. To me, it would make perfect sense for people to think that's where the birth of the nation started. I think Ozzie should veer north and head toward the City of Brotherly Shove."

"It's Love, Stan," Brook said.

"We're from Brooklyn. When I'm referring to Philadelphia, I say *shove*. Nick gets it."

"Yeah, sure," Nick said. "Glad you paid attention in your US history class, Stan."

"You kidding me? I just jumped on the Internet."

"Fine. But we can't look at this through a single lens."

"Agreed, but I think Stan's taking the right approach," I interjected. "Less guessing, more gathering of facts. Denise and I did the same thing when we were sitting in LAX trying to figure out the answer to the first riddle."

A momentary pause in speaking. I looked at the phone to make sure the line hadn't disconnected.

"That gives me another idea, Ozzie," Nick said.

"And that is?"

"When Stan first called me to discuss the situation, my first thought was to bring in an FBI colleague and probably my closest friend, Alex Troutt."

I could feel my body tense up. "Why, Nick? I know you're very experienced; you were even at Camp Israel, helped save all of those people, from what I read. Are you not confident in your abilities?"

"It's not that. Well, kind of. We have very little time. We need to decipher this riddle. But the fact they chose Camp Israel for this last production, I think, is very significant."

"So what does this Alex guy have that you don't have?"

"It's a she. And her mother was held captive at Camp Israel for over thirty years. She's the one who pushed us to get into that camp, to save those people. Without Alex, there would have been a massive slaughter of people. As it was, she lost her mom. It was tragic, but she knows her shit better than anyone."

I looked at the long, dark road ahead of me. We'd been on the phone for just a few minutes, and to a degree, it seemed like none of them knew more than I did. Probably a harsh assessment, but the pressure inside me was reaching a boiling point.

"Bring her in, Nick," I said.

Thirty-Four

The moment I heard Alex speak, something made me pause. The timbre of her voice sounded familiar somehow. Within seconds, I could sense her obvious leadership qualities. "I need a complete status," she said, a roaring sound in the background. "But give it to me in thirty seconds, Nick. Go."

Nick did just that, and he did it with remarkable accuracy and brevity.

"Ozzie, first of all, I can't tell how you how sorry I am to hear what happened to Denise," Alex said. "I'm sure you're feeling about a hundred different things right now. I've been there. We're not going to leave your side. We will figure this out."

And just like that, I felt another rush of emotion. It was for Denise, for the desperation of finding Mackenzie, and for people, basically strangers, saying they had my back.

"Much appreciated, Alex. Any ideas on this riddle? The clock is ticking, and we're not sure where I should go."

Another roar from the phone. It sounded distorted. I turned down my hearing aid a bit.

"Sorry. I'm at Luke's basketball game. Let me get out into the hallway."

It sounded like she asked someone to come along with her, but I couldn't be certain.

"So, Oz, Nick was right to bring me in. He told you about my connection to Camp Israel, yes?"

"He did. I can't imagine what you went through for all those years."

"It was crazy, I'll grant you that. I'm bringing it up because of this first part of this new riddle. *Where the Prophet was first swaddled.* Taking Camp Israel out of the equation, you might think of someone from the Bible or some other religion. Putting Camp Israel back into the equation, when you think about it, Moses wasn't born in Maryland. So it makes sense that they're not referencing anyone from two thousand years ago. This has to be more recent."

"Malachi?"

It was another man's voice.

"Who is that?" I quickly asked. "Nick, did you add someone else to this call without me knowing?"

"Not me. I think that sounds like—"

"Sorry, Oz," Alex said. "My, uh, boyfriend, Brad, is right here next to me."

I immediately felt steam coming off my head. "I thought we were keeping this just between us. Now we're adding in boyfriends. What's next? Video streaming live on Facebook?"

A moment of silence.

"Hey, Oz. Brad is cool," Nick said.

"I'm sure he's Joe Cool. It just makes me nervous, that's all. The larger the group, the higher the likelihood of something getting out."

"Nothing will get out," Alex said. "I guarantee you that."

Another definitive comment from the boss lady. I didn't respond.

She continued. "Ozzie, look. We want you to get your daughter. I'm willing to halt everything I'm doing to make that happen. But Nick knew this would come up. We have a tight group of people we work with here, and I trust all of them with my life. They've come through every time. Without question."

"No offense, but your boyfriend? I mean, what's he going to do? Make you coffee? Rub your feet?"

I thought I detected a sigh. Might have been more crowd noise.

"Oz," Brook said, "give her a chance, dude. This is our best hope."

"Okay, okay. Talk to me."

"Brad is my boyfriend, yes, but he's also the best damn intelligence analyst the FBI has."

Now it made sense. The ultimate office romance. *How long will that last?* I wondered but dared not say.

"Okay, so Brad knows his shit. I guess you can add him to the mix."

"There's one more person we need to involve," Alex said.

"Don't tell me. Your son isn't just a kid playing basketball; he's got superhuman powers like one of the kids in *The Incredibles*."

"Damn, you're snarky," Stan said.

"Sounds just like Alex," Nick added. "The queen of sarcasm."

"Me or her?" I said, almost laughing. "Forget it."

"Are you guys done yet?" Alex asked. "So, the person I want to bring in is a technical wizard. On top of that, her brain essentially operates like a supercomputer. Her name is Gretchen. She's our top SOS."

"SOS," I said. "That seems appropriate." There were a couple of snickers at that one.

"Nick, can you—"

"I'm sending Gretchen a text right now," he said.

It was like watching the Justice League assemble before my very eyes.

"Now, can we get past our team and move on to the business of getting your daughter back?"

"Please." I pulled my fingers from the steering wheel and wiped them on my jeans. Hands back on the wheel, I did a little stretch of my back; it felt like a pole had been inserted in my spine. I tried to relax, but it didn't do much to ease the stabbing pain.

"Back to the riddle. We were talking about the Prophet and how I think it might be connected to Camp Israel."

"I got that part. What about Malachi? That's a book from the Old Testament, I think," I said.

"It is, but he was also the leader of the group at Camp Israel."

"Is this Brad?" I asked.

"That's me, yes."

"Brad, two things," Alex said. "First, I need you to find out where Malachi, a.k.a. Eldridge Kaufman, was born. Second, after that, we need to figure out what federal prison he's in and make sure he's still there."

I was about to speak up, but Alex had one more order. "Wait. Before all that, go find Erin. Tell her she needs to bring Luke home after the game. Guys and Brook, Brad and I will start to head home. We'll stay on the line, but we'll work better from there."

"I didn't know Erin was driving on her own," Nick said. "I mean, she's only sixteen."

"That's the legal age to drive, Nick," Alex said sharply. "She stays close to home and can drive with no more than one friend in the car. I just hope she can get Luke home without them starting World War III. But that's a normal problem."

The line was silent for a few seconds. It sounded like the wheels were in motion to make progress. But where it would take us, if it would get me to this mystery location by the deadline, I had no idea. My confidence level right now wavered anywhere between ten and ninety percent, depending on the thoughts flashing through my mind at any given moment.

I was now on Route 28. I saw a sign for Hopeville, only five miles away. It seemed like I was making good time. The Beast was holding up. Virgil had come through for me, which was amazing, considering I'd pulled a gun on the guy. I'd come to the conclusion that there were people in this world who really cared about others. They tried to do the right thing, even if it wasn't popular with the locals—or, as was the case with Nick, Alex, and their team, even if they weren't following strict FBI protocol. How could I ever repay them? If we got Mackenzie back, I'd figure out something.

"I'm here. How can I help?"

It was a female voice. Actually, it sounded like a chirping bird.

"That's Gretchen," Nick said. "Welcome, Gretchen."

"Thanks. I know the routine. I'm sitting at my workstation right now. I don't know much about what's going on, but just tell me what you need done. I can get the details later."

"Hey, Gretchen," Brad said, and then I heard what sounded like a car door shutting. "Let's split up the tasks. We need the birthplace of Eldridge Kaufman."

"If memory serves me correctly, he'd done a pretty decent job of covering his past," Gretchen said. "But it's got to be attached to his court case through the US Attorney's Office, if nothing else. Let me see what I can do."

Brad said he was jumping on his phone to make sure this Kaufman guy was still in prison.

Stan and Brook said they'd continue brainstorming on ideas for solving the riddle. "I know this might sound stupid," Brook said, "But Stan and I are here in Texas. Actually, he's in San Antonio, and I'm in Austin. Anything you guys think we need to follow up on here?"

"I actually grew up there," Alex said.

Well, that was a surprise. "Small world and all, I guess," I said. "What part?"

"Along the coast, little town called Port Isabel. Haven't been back since my dad died."

I thought more about Alex's mom and how she'd been held by this lunatic for three decades. I was curious, and I wanted to ask more questions. Later, maybe.

"Wow," Brook said, "I guess all roads really do lead to Texas."

Alex didn't say anything, which told me there was still some pain related to her dad's death or just her upbringing, not having a mom around. Again, I'd been lucky to have been adopted by my family. Dysfunctional, for certain, but somewhere at least close to the normal zone, comparatively speaking.

"Ozzie," Alex finally said, "I know this might be painful, but tell me more about what you found at Camp Israel."

I exhaled and tried to distance myself from the emotion. I described the eeriness of the hushed compound and then the Jeep that I saw drive off into the woods.

"Gretchen, I know you're hunting for Kaufman's birthplace, but mark that down about the Jeep. Might need to cross-reference that against another data point."

"Got it."

"Continue, Ozzie," Alex said.

I recounted the whole story, the sheets of plastic, the wind blowing, and then finding Denise with her eyes open. As much as I tried not to go there, tears welled in my eyes. "Guys, is there any way we can get her body out of there and give her a proper burial? I mean, she's just lying there under a sheet I found."

"Of course. Nick, can you try to figure out how to get that done?"

"I'm on it."

Stan said, "Tell Alex about the video you saw, Oz."

"I know it's painful, but it might be helpful," Brook said.

"What video? No one told me about any video." Alex's intensity had gone up a notch, I could tell.

I wasn't happy at having to relive that moment again, but I sucked it up and described every detail I'd watched and heard on the video.

"Jesus H. Christ," Nick said in a hushed tone.

"Thank you, Ozzie," Alex said. "Nick, is there any way we can call up Vandiver in the nearby FBI office? Maybe he can help get the body out of there without too much attention. But what I really want is the video. Ozzie said there might have been a frame or two that picked up the face of one of these Neanderthals."

I put a hand in my pocket. "Guys, I have the video card with me right here."

"No shit?" Brook blurted out. "Why didn't you tell us?"

"Forgot about it. And on top of that, what good is it? I can't slide it in my phone and email the video."

And that was when our small team took it to a completely different level.

Thirty-Five

The rumble of the airplane engines, seemingly almost on top of me, momentarily rattled the ancient dashboard inside the Beast. I could also feel it in my chest, which made my heart skip a beat.

Damn, my nerves were fried.

I zoomed into Dulles Airport, on the west side of DC, the road and surrounding sea of concrete bathed in light—the exact opposite of ninety percent of my trip coming in from Elkins, West Virginia. My eyes were on constant alert, even though I knew there was a plan. I'd caught the name of the street I was driving on—Autopilot Drive. I wasn't sure if that was some type of pathetic attempt at irony; of course, logically, I knew the sign hadn't been erected just in the last few hours to play with my mind.

I pushed out a deep breath. The world was not out to get me. Just some unknown group of people had made it their mission to murder my girlfriend from ten years ago and steal away a daughter I never knew I had.

Based on my last call with the team, we'd all but ruled out the *yakuza*. Nothing was certain, Alex had said. So, she put the likelihood of *yakuza* involvement at around thirty percent, although she couldn't explain the series of events at the front end of this nightmarish debacle. It was difficult to connect what had happened in Hawaii with what was happening now.

Even after being on the phone for most of the last two hours with Alex, Nick, Brad, Gretchen, Stan, and Brook, questions still peppered my mind. Most could be rolled up into two words: Who? Why?

I'd ponder those once I boarded the plane that was due to take off in approximately thirty-five minutes. Traffic slowed near the terminals. I picked up an old magazine from the floorboard, wrapped my pistol in it, and stuffed it behind the bench seat.

I pulled up to the valet station at the main terminal, swapped my keys for a paper card, and hoped that someday soon I'd be able to return the pickup to Virgil. It had served its purpose. Before I made it to the door, I felt crystals of freezing rain dropping on my head. It only added to my anxiety of making it to my destination on time.

In the terminal, I found an open station at the United Airlines counter. I told the agent I was running behind to make my departure time. The ticket had already been purchased by Alex's team, and within three minutes, I was headed toward the security line. Once there, I veered toward the frequent-traveler line. As expected, it was much shorter, and people were moving through at record speed. Somehow, Gretchen had put me on the list. I didn't ask how. I was just thankful. The process went smoothly, and I hustled toward Concourse C. But I didn't go straight there. Even though I was worried they wouldn't let me on the flight, I stayed on task, in accordance with our plan.

I found the Dunkin' Donuts in Concourse A, purchased a small cup of ice—yes, they made me pay a dollar for it—and walked over to a water fountain. I popped the lid off the top, tilted my head back, chewed on some ice, and nonchalantly dumped the rest of the ice in the water fountain. As I fit the lid back on, I slipped the video card inside the cup. I pretended to take a pull from the straw, then left the cup on a table next to the first chair nearest the walkway at gate A21.

As much as I wanted to glance around and look for this Brad person, I kept my eyes straight ahead and made a beeline toward Concourse C. I hustled up to gate C14 as the last-call announcement was being made over the speaker system. The agent scanned my ticket, and I ambled down the ramp. I squeezed my body into seat 22B—a middle seat, which for someone of my height and girth, was cruel. Glancing up, I watched as more passengers followed behind me. Four men, two kids, and three women. Which one was Brad?

It was better I didn't know, I was told. If someone was watching, we couldn't let them know that the FBI was now involved. Heavily.

I looked around the person to my right and glanced outside the tiny window. The glow of a spotlight illuminated a light sheet of precipitation, probably frozen. I took out my phone and checked the timer. If the plane was forced to go through a de-icing process, I'd be screwed. There would be no way for me to get to my destination, pick up my rental, and drive the hour and nine minutes.

Looking toward the front of the plane, I could see a mom holding her child in one arm and trying to put a carry-on bag in the overhead. The kid, who looked to be about two, was red-faced, kicking and bucking. It made sense—it was after nine o'clock at night. He was probably tired and wanted no part of this trip.

The woman struggled for a good twenty seconds. No one stepped in to help her. Everyone had their heads buried in some device, many of them wearing earbuds, lost in their own worlds.

"Excuse me." I pushed up, banged my head off the low ceiling, and looked at the person to my left. The girl slouched in her chair, earbuds in, eyes closed, smacking her gum. She had two red dreadlocks tied behind her head. She kind of reminded me of my friend Poppy back in Austin.

I tapped her knee. "Excuse me," I said again. She moved her legs, although she acted like I'd asked her to skydive out of a plane at forty thousand feet without a parachute.

I scooted into the aisle and quickly made my way to the woman and child. "Here, let me get that for you."

"Oh…" She seemed surprised but relieved. She picked up her boy, who immediately hushed and put his face against her shoulder.

I placed her carry-on in the bin and shut it.

"Rodney, can you tell the man 'thank you'?" she said to the boy.

I saw his green eyes peek out from his mom's chest. He almost smiled and then quickly turned away.

"He's just shy."

"And tired maybe."

"Yes," she said with a heavy sigh. "Do you have little kids you're going home to?" She was looking at my left hand.

My jaw opened, but no words came out. I didn't know what to say, exactly. Thoughts of Denise came to mind, Mackenzie, and then they circled back to Nicole—my wife, who was living in what I used to call our home.

Home. I wasn't sure I could pinpoint my home. Not just in terms of an address, either.

"Sorry if I hit a sore subject."

"No, I'm just tired. Ready to get…home."

I made it back into my seat, and within seconds, the captain told us he was preparing for liftoff before the weather took a turn for the worse. I unlocked my phone and found Mackenzie's picture, the one Denise had sent me when we were speaking with

Hulama. Her mischievous smile with a missing tooth made me shake my head. There were familiar things about her too. It was surreal to look at someone and see part of yourself.

"Is that your daughter?"

I turned to my left as the girl sat up in her seat, pulled out her earbuds.

I paused a second, glanced back at Mackenzie's picture, then looked at the girl. "Yeah, that's my daughter."

"That's cool."

It was indeed.

Thirty-Six

The plane bounced onto the runway at Logan Airport, and after a brief ride, we pulled up to the gate. The captain spoke as passengers scurried about in the aisles: "Welcome to the home of Paul Revere." He said if anyone was just visiting the city of Boston, he highly recommended going on the Freedom Trail.

Freedom. That was exactly why I was here—to secure Mackenzie's freedom. I glanced at the timer on my phone. The plane had arrived four minutes early. But I had no more than fifteen minutes to depart the plane, rent my car, and head south out of Boston.

My destination was a small, foreclosed home in the southern part of Plymouth. Yes, home of Plymouth Rock. The key to figuring out the riddle went back to Camp Israel and this Malachi person who had led the religious cult. Alex had quickly taken us down the correct path.

I learned that Eldridge Kaufman was considered a prophet by those in his brainwashed clan. Then Gretchen dug up information on his first home; it was near the intersection of Old Sandwich and State in Plymouth. From there, it made sense that Boston, or Plymouth specifically, could be referenced as the place where the nation was first formed.

I was damn lucky to have Alex and her small team on my side. My stubbornness could have…

I stopped my thought before I got there and eyed the organized chaos of people departing the plane. A man in a suit helped the woman I'd met earlier pull down her carry-on bag. Her little boy, Rodney, had his head once again on her shoulder. He was fast asleep, which I found astonishing. Kids. There was so much I didn't know.

I scooted into the aisle, but, similar to the flight from LAX into DC, I had to wait on folks in the front as they lazily got their stuff together. The crush of people behind me apparently didn't see the foot traffic slow down, and I was sandwiched.

"Dude, give me some space please," I said to the guy who'd gone well inside my personal space.

"Sorry," he said, finally backing up a step.

With my frustration nearing the red zone, I looked toward the exit. I was almost ready to start shoving people aside when a flight attendant jumped into action and ushered people off with surprising efficiency.

I marched up the ramp, spotted an arrow to the car-rental area, and headed in that direction. I raced up to the company with the green sign and gave them my name. Again, a reservation was waiting for me, and the typically long checkout process was completed in mere seconds. I walked out the door and was met with a blast of cold wind that made my eyes water. A blue shuttle was at the curb. I got on the bus and was delivered to the parking lot. Three minutes later, I jumped into the black Buick and screeched out of the lot. Once I was out of the airport, I dialed the secure line.

"Ozzie, is that you?" It was Brook.

"I'm here, in my car, about ready to get onto I-90."

Brook said, "Hallelujah. You made it."

"He still has a ways to go."

That was Alex. Apparently, optimism wasn't in her DNA.

"Brook, I should be okay, right? My timer says we have an hour and ten minutes. I'm five minutes ahead of that pace."

"You don't know Boston traffic."

"Is that Nick?"

"Who else do you think it is?"

"Your cousin maybe."

"Oh, Stan had to drop out for now. His kid had an episode."

More kid stuff. I wondered if there was an online guide on how to proactively deal with these so-called "episodes," as it were. Later, I'd research it, once I had Mackenzie.

I saw the road dip down toward a tunnel.

"By the way, you might lose us when you…"

The line went dead as I powered the Buick into the tunnel. I was crossing the Boston Harbor. I smelled car exhaust, but I also picked up the scent of the ocean. I came out on the south side. The largest part of the skyline was on my right. I saw signs for Beacon Hill, Back Bay, the Boston Opera House, and even the Freedom Trail. The road turned into I-93. I dialed back into the line and heard Nick's voice.

"I want to raid the house right now, even before Ozzie gets there. He could be walking into a trap."

"No way," I said.

"Didn't hear you rejoin the call," Alex said.

"If you guys do that, they might see you coming. They could kill Mackenzie."

"They could kill you. In fact, I think they *will* try to kill you, Ozzie," Nick said. "What other reason could they have for luring you to that place? I want to be wrong. But nothing else would make sense."

I wiped a hand across my face, trying to take in everything he'd just relayed. Confusion and doubt began to take hold of my thoughts. "Dammit, Alex, I thought we were clear."

"Look, Ozzie, we all bring something to the table. It's not personal."

"Do you believe your partner?"

A hesitation. "It's very possible, yes. As you know, I have kids. They mean the world to me. I'd do anything for them, even if I had to cross the line of the law."

"Hell, you have done it," Nick chimed in.

"Anyway, the risk of something bad happening if we raid the house is real. But there's also a risk if we don't. You've got to know that."

My whole body broke out in a sweat. It was up to me to make the call. I just wanted Mackenzie back...safely. I punched the window button, and it slid down a few inches until the chilled air swept across my face.

"Are you and Nick already there?"

"We're about ten minutes out. But if I call this in to my SSA, then I'm sure I can have at least a couple other agents meet us there within thirty minutes. Maybe more than two."

"What's an SSA?"

"It's just my boss, Jerry. He's cool."

I weaved through a bit of traffic, trying to take everything in. "So, if we don't call in the cavalry, you and Nick would be positioned close by, right? Like you said earlier?"

"Yep. There's a tiny little road just south of the home. It's a dead-end street just off State Road. Quiet and dark. By car, it's maybe thirty seconds away from where you'll be."

I considered that. "Okay, let's stick with the original plan. It just seems right. I can keep the line open on my cell phone. It might be muffled, but I could yell out something if things go bad."

"You think they're going to announce it?" Nick said. "Sheesh, Ozzie. You don't even have a weapon on you. You could be lights out before you take one step into the house."

"We could get him a weapon," Alex said.

That sounded like it was a question for Nick.

"It's possible. If there's enough time, we could meet someplace close to the house—but not too close."

"What do you think, Ozzie?" Alex said. "Are you comfortable using a sidearm?"

"I'd rather have one than not, but I also don't want to create a conflict by having one." I sighed and felt a twinge of pain in my chest, as if someone had pinched a corner of my heart. As I scratched around the area, a quick thought of my dad and his heart issues flashed in and out of my mind. "Like everything else, Alex, at this point, I'm confused which way to go, anxious that I'll make the wrong call."

"Okay, we don't have to decide this second. Nick is on his phone right now, trying to find a quick handoff location. You still have about forty-five minutes of driving."

Handoff. "Hey, did your boyfriend ever get the cup with the video card?"

"Boyfriend is on the line."

"And so is Gretchen."

I couldn't mistake her voice.

"And even though I can't do a whole lot, Brook is here too." A familiar voice.

"I have the video card, and I'm almost at Gretchen's apartment," Brad said.

He must have been one of the four men I saw jump on the plane at the last second. "Brad, everyone, you guys operate better than the Longhorns basketball team."

"Did you go to UT?" Alex asked.

"For a bit. Long story. Graduated undergrad from Cal-Berkeley."

"I went to UT," she said.

It made sense, since she'd grown up on the coast, but it still was a crazy coincidence. No one spoke for a moment, so I jumped in with, "Well, I'm not sure what kind of magic you can do with the video before I get to the house."

More silence. I hated silence, and not only because of my hearing issues. "Did I use the wrong code word or something?"

A clearing of the throat. "Let's just say we believe it's prudent to work multiple angles in parallel," Alex said.

"I think you're trying to say Gretchen needs to try to work the video angle in case Mackenzie isn't at the house in Plymouth. Am I right?"

"I didn't want to say it, but yes."

"If I take a step back and think more like a lawyer and less like someone who—"

"You're a lawyer?" Alex's voice was nearing Gretchen's soprano level.

"Yes. Kind of. Probably not much longer."

"That's so weird. I used to be a lawyer," she said. "I hated it, so I joined the FBI, hoping to make a real difference and not just sit in a stuffy office and play footsy with a bunch of suits."

As I processed the odd similarities in our lives, I veered onto Route 3 and immediately saw a line of red brake lights. I banged the steering wheel.

"Looks like we won't have time for the weapon handoff after all," I said.

Thirty-Seven

The house was barely visible from State Road as I passed by it. Not a single light was on. I saw no one on the property, which was just a little larger than an acre, from what Gretchen had shared. Trees outlined the small, one-story home, which was set back about two hundred feet from the road.

I parked just around the corner on Treetop Way. When I exited the car, I quietly shut the door. It made no sense, really. It was ten minutes after eleven, so they should be expecting me. I traipsed through weeds and leaves, making it to the front yard before pausing for a moment. The home was only fifteen hundred square feet, again from Gretchen. The exterior was a forgettable gray stone. Brick steps led up to a tiny front porch. The wooden handrail leaned out about forty-five degrees.

I touched the phone in my back pocket. The conference line was still open, although I had no idea how much they'd be able to hear. Regardless of what Nick had said, I still believed I could grab the phone and yell into it, signaling them to get to the house. "Thirty seconds" was what Alex had said.

I picked up a strong scent of pine needles as I tiptoed through the front lawn and up the steps. I stopped right there, unsure if I should knock or just walk in. There was no doorbell. I reached for the doorknob and immediately realized the door was cracked open. My mouth went dry.

It was darker inside than outside. After I did a quick look-see behind me, I gradually pushed the door open and took a step inside. My foot landed with a thud. I'd forgotten that Gretchen had said it was a pier-and-beam home. So, the echo of my step made sense. I brought my other foot in and paused. The place seemed empty. No sign of people anywhere. But there was plenty of silence. Until…

"I'm glad you made it, Dad."

The girl's voice sent a jolt up my spine. I swallowed, tried to keep my composure. "Mackenzie, is that you?"

No immediate response. I wasn't exactly sure of the origin of the sound. I scanned the empty space. My eyes had adjusted somewhat to the darkness. I could make out a bar counter in front of me. Was she in the kitchen?

"Mackenzie?"

Still nothing. I worried about my ability to pick up the slightest of sounds. But I couldn't just stand there and wait. I walked on my toes toward the counter. I could feel the loose padding of carpet under my shoes.

"Dad, I've been waiting to see you. I've always wanted to meet you."

I stopped. I was no more than five feet from the counter. I tried to swallow, but my throat was practically clamped shut. So many emotions. Hearing my daughter speak…of me. I felt an instant connection, an unyielding desire to find her, to protect her.

"Mackenzie, I'm here. Where are you?"

I couldn't hear a sound. I took a single step and placed my hand on the counter, which was covered with dust. My eyes were drawn to a small window on the far side of the kitchen, where a small bit of light seeped in. The sink that should have been under the window wasn't there. Someone must have stolen it.

I circled around the counter, leaning forward to get a full view of the kitchen floor. The far side was pitch black. I blinked, thinking I saw a figure there, huddled in the corner. "Mackenzie, is that you?"

A thud behind me rippled through the hollow floors into my feet. I flipped my head around. I saw the fist a split second before it connected with the bridge of my nose. Motes of light danced above my head as I stumbled backward. The only thing that stopped me was the counter. Then I crumbled to the floor.

I pushed up to my hands and knees, wobbling, barely able to keep my balance. Some type of laughter near me. I looked toward the dark corner. Was Mackenzie over there, possibly tied up?

A second later, two quick thuds—as if someone was getting a running start—and a heavy boot rammed into my rib cage. I fell to my side as unbridled pain shot through my core. For a moment, I couldn't breathe. I began to panic. My lung must have collapsed.

Hands grabbed my shirt, pulled me up to standing. This new position somehow released the pinch in my lungs. I inhaled, exhaled. Instant relief. Another fist headed in my direction, and I ducked, but the punch still popped my collarbone, the same one I'd broken in Pee Wee football. This time, it felt more like a stab. *That wasn't just a fist*, I surmised. Something was on the fist, maybe brass knuckles.

Down on one knee, one more breath. I swung my head in both directions. A guy behind me, one more approaching me. No idea if Mackenzie was in the corner or where they might have her.

Where the hell were Alex and Nick?

My phone. I reached around to my pocket. My fingers brushed against broken glass and metal. Just my luck.

A chuckle from above me. "You see, Mickey, this twit's got nothing. He's not only mortal, he's sub-mortal."

A machine gun of laughter from my other side. "Joseph way overestimated this guy. He's nothing special. No great superpowers. Let's just do the world a favor and kill him like all the others. What do you say, Tanner?"

They were reveling in their dominance over me. I blinked a couple of times. My mind was crawling out of the cobwebs just enough.

I whipped my leg around like a gymnast on the horse and cracked Mickey on the outside of his knee. He let out some type of primal groan and began to topple over. Using my momentum, I continued my three-sixty turn and put all of my weight behind a right hand to Tanner's solar plexus.

I could hear the air leaving his lungs as he folded, stumbled backward. I turned and saw Mickey moving toward the dark corner.

"Leave her alone!" I yelled, hurling my body in that direction. I collided with Mickey, and we both slammed into a chair and then a wall. No Mackenzie. Where the hell was she?

Mickey and I were face to face; he was heaving out breaths. I could feel his spit on my neck. He had something in his hand, struggling to move it upward. I was throwing punches but also trying to stop his arms from moving.

My hand brushed across something metal. A gun.

A surge of adrenaline shot through my extremities. I tried grabbing his arms, holding him against the wall. He was quick, though. He flailed violently, trying to free himself. We tussled, both fighting for control of the gun. I couldn't get my hands around his fist. At one point, I even hopped backward because I thought he was about to shoot my leg. That extra space was all he needed. He jabbed a knee into my groin. Partial connection—but any connection was not good. I could feel the shock of pain deep in my stomach. It instantly sapped my energy, made me want to vomit. I got dizzy, dropped my arms to my knees. It was as if I had no control of my body.

I caught a glint of light bouncing off his gun as he brought the weapon to his chest. Summoning strength from some unknown source, I swung my arms up just as the gun fired. Glass and dust rained on me. The bullet had hit the ceiling, maybe an overhead light fixture.

The shot had stunned both of us, it seemed. But his midsection was now exposed. I threw a left hook into his ribs. He doubled over, but that just made my right uppercut connect with his chin with even more velocity. His teeth clattered. I saw one of his hands fall to his side.

I reached for his gun hand, but he head-butted me. More motes of light. I could now smell blood in the air. A couple of blinks, and I lunged for his gun hand. He started flailing again but with less energy. I could feel the pistol, but his sweaty hand slipped out of my grip. The gun turned upward, aimed right at my gut.

I knew at this moment it was all or nothing. He'd shoot me in the stomach, and then he and his buddy would laugh as I spilled blood until I died. Or they might kick me around just for the fun of it. They might even just get it over with and put a bullet in my head. Either way, I saw my life flash before my eyes. It had all started with Mackenzie. My daughter. The little girl whose voice I'd heard. I had no idea what they'd done to her. She had to be scared. Would they kill her? I had no clue what this was all about.

More images zipped across my mind. I saw Denise on our prom date. She had on this strapless dress, a silver number that showed off her shoulders and chest but also made her blue eyes sparkle. I'd liked her before that night, but her eyes, her aura, drew me in like never before. We danced, partied with our friends, but our connection, at least for that one night, was unlike anything I'd experienced in my life. We wanted each other in the most primal way, and we showed it once we got to our hotel room. The night Mackenzie was conceived.

I jumped to Denise in Hawaii. She was a histrionic mess; who wouldn't be if their child had just been kidnapped? But I also saw her demons nibbling at the frayed edges of her sanity. I wanted to help her, to undo everything that had been done, but it wasn't possible. I had done my best to help. Yet I couldn't keep her from being killed. I'd left her at the apparel shop, believing it would keep her out of harm's way. But it had all backfired. It was as though they—this organization or group that had somehow tracked us all the way from Hawaii—knew that I'd leave her behind.

The video. They'd slapped her, put a gun to her head. Made her overdose on drugs. And they made me watch it.

My life in Austin. Dad had died just a week earlier; Mom was going through some type of crisis. The law firm with my name on it was probably officially shut down by now.

Nicole. She was to be my "forever." She might lament my death, but maybe it would be best for her in the long run. To start anew and recapture that magic with someone else.

Back to the moment. I prepared for a bullet to the gut.

I closed my eyes, but I didn't hear a pop or feel a stabbing pain. Instead, I heard a loud slam just as huge hands grabbed my shoulders. I opened my eyes. Mickey had turned to the front of the house. But the other guy had his paws on me. I jabbed my elbow into his throat, snatched the gun out of Mickey's hand, turned, and was about to shoot when I saw two figures enter the kitchen, shouting.

Alex and Nick?

Tanner charged at them. Two shots were fired. He brought a hand to his chest, tripped, and fell until his head bounced off the floor.

"You okay, Ozzie?" Alex asked.

I whipped around. A flashlight from over my shoulder, from either Alex or Nick, cast a cone of light on Mickey. He was on the floor, a hand near his mouth.

He said, "Whoever seeks to keep his life will lose it, and whoever loses his life will preserve it."

I was still processing these words when he slipped something into his mouth. Nick rushed by me, dropping to the floor.

"No, dammit!" Nick said, swiping at the guy's arm. He turned his head to look up at Alex and me. "I think he just swallowed some type of pill."

A moment later, as Nick called for paramedics, the thug started foaming at the mouth. He collapsed. Dead.

As the sirens approached the house, I put both palms on the counter. A gentle hand fell on my shoulder. I turned to see Alex. "Where's Mackenzie?" I asked, my voice quaking.

"She's not here, Ozzie." She held up a device of some kind, maybe an iPad. "It was all a hoax."

Thirty-Eight

Joseph flicked the pen between his two fingers and searched his mind for just the right words to add to the speech he was writing. A million phrases came to mind, but he knew this speech had to be unlike any other. It had to deliver the type of message that would earmark his legacy and begin a tidal wave of change.

He pulled back the burlap curtain and peeked out the small window of his hut. A few people scattered about the camp to ensure the proper security was in place, but most had turned in for the night.

It had been difficult to concentrate over the last six hours, but the last fifteen minutes had been excruciating.

As the leader of the Kingdom, as the sole purveyor of His word, he knew that he didn't have the luxury of delaying the upcoming event. It wasn't even possible. This event would be the culmination of a year of deep reflection and planning. But what made it so meaningful was that it would come after a lifetime of listless wandering, searching for that sole purpose of why he was put on this earth.

One year ago, when he'd received the very first correspondence, he came to understand his purpose. It was all meant to be. Fate.

He put his pen to paper, puckered his lips, and pushed out a gentle breath. His creative ideas flowed more easily when he was in the zone, seeking that nearly utopian place that channeled divine wisdom at a level he'd not yet experienced. Yes, he'd read about such a communicator, a supreme leader, but had never seen it with his own two eyes or felt it in his gut.

That would soon change, which was why, deep inside, he was almost giddy with excitement. They were so very close to making this happen.

Focus, Joseph.

He'd penned only a few more words when his door opened. In walked Cecelia, her face etched with a refrained enthusiasm. Her cheeks had a pink glow, although he knew that could be from their earlier encounter, one in which she'd not only pleasured him in a way no other woman could but also had reaffirmed her faith in his wisdom, in his sheer greatness.

She lifted onto her toes, as she curled a lock of hair around her ear.

"Speak, Cecelia. Please," he said, raising his arm.

"I've just received the call from Paul, and he said it happened just like you said it would. He saw it with his own eyes while looking through the back window. Mickey and Tanner, as you predicted, were not able to fend off his strength. The other two, though, came in and helped him. Does that make him less desirable?"

He shook his head and rolled the pen between his hands. "It was as I envisioned," he said, recalling this very same prediction from his supreme leader.

She was back on her toes again, and he moved his arm lower. "Let us bow our heads and think of the sacrifices made by our brothers, Mickey and Tanner."

"Oh, right."

They lowered their heads for a moment of silence, although his eyes went back to his speech. Words were flooding his mind. He needed to put them on paper. But that would have to wait.

"I'd like to make one more visit to our special guest. But as I gather my things, please initiate the next phase. It is all lined up, correct?"

"Just as we've discussed for weeks."

"Very well," he said, nodding his head for her to proceed.

She turned her back to him, put the phone to her ear. He took his time putting on his robe, then glanced at himself in the small mirror inside his bureau. He shut the doors. She was standing there, brimming with excitement.

"All is in motion?"

"Yes. I just need to make one more call. Our most important call."

He rested his hand on her arm. "Patience, Cecelia. Let us walk together over to the pen and relay the good news."

They walked outside, passed a single member of the tribe, who dipped his head in respect. They both reciprocated. They continued their trek, weaving around workstations and the garden, beyond the area used for defecation and fertilization. By the last lit torch, they stopped at a pit dug into the rocky hillside. It was reinforced and barricaded with rebar.

Cecelia lowered to her knees, as Joseph peered over her back into the darkness of the pit.

"Mackenzie, we have arrived with good news."

It took a few seconds, but a little girl's face appeared from the darkness. Her eyes were, unsurprisingly, wide with fear. "Yes?" her voice cracked.

"It will only be a matter of hours before your father joins you. And then you and he will be joined together forever in salvation." Joseph couldn't withhold his smile.

"What about Mom? Is Mom coming too?"

Cecelia suddenly put her hands on the cage. Was she reaching out, trying to comfort the child? He tried to ignore it. He released a slow breath, rested his hands on his knees. "We've told you before that your mother has already begun the ascension of her afterlife. You should be joyous."

The little girl blinked a few times but held her gaze. He studied her. Was she being defiant?

He could feel a heat invade his neck, but he withheld the need to scold her. Instead, he thought about the strong will that ran through her bloodline, and yes, her father included.

Tonight, blood would be spilled, and blood would be imbibed. And two sacrifices would be made. The ultimate sacrifices that would achieve his goal: to bring the essence of his supreme leader into his body, into his soul, so that he could carry this cause to the rest of the world.

Omnipotence would soon be his.

Thirty-Nine

I had barely moved in the last few minutes. Even with lights shining all around me, and cops and paramedics bustling nearby—all their clamoring was nothing more than white noise—I found it hard to take my eyes off the counter.

A hoax. This whole thing had been a setup to bring me to Plymouth, Massachusetts. To tease me into thinking Mackenzie was here, wanting for me, her father, to finally save her from the heathens who had kidnapped her. Their goal was to take me to the edge of hope and then yank it away. They wanted to torment me. And then to kill me.

Nick and Alex appeared at my side.

"Ozzie, I know you're not in a good place right now, but I wish you'd let the paramedics treat your wounds," Alex said.

I kept my eyes on the counter.

"Ozzie?" Her hand touched my arm.

I turned my head and looked straight at her. Her blue eyes. For a second, it was like looking in a mirror…similar to the feeling I'd had when looking at Mackenzie's picture. A few lines tugged at the edges of her eyes. I could tell she'd lived through pain and torment of her own, but I got the sense she was not just a survivor, but one who didn't let the past define her.

"I'll be okay. Any idea who these guys were, beyond just the names of Mickey and Tanner?" I removed my hands from the counter. I could taste blood at the edge of my lips.

"No identification on either one," Nick said as his eyes wandered over to the medical examiner stooped over the guy who'd taken the pill.

I did a double-take on Nick—and not because of his thick Brooklyn accent. He had his hands at his waist, under a suit coat and suspenders. He was older than Alex but in good shape.

I turned and rested my backside against the counter, but I felt a sharp stab in my ribs. "I just don't understand—" I stopped short, unable to relay what I was thinking and feeling.

"It's beyond cruel, Ozzie," Alex said, shaking her head. "But dammit, it's not over. We still have hope."

"Hope. I think I've forgotten what that word means." I ran my hand across my face. Wrong move. It brushed across my cut from that asshole's brass knuckles.

"You're really hurt, Oz. You look like you've been in a cage fight, and I saw you grab at your ribs. Let me get a paramedic back in here."

I ignored her request. "You said it wasn't over. Why do you think that?"

"First, a question." She held up a clear baggie that contained the iPad. "Can you confirm if that was Mackenzie's voice?"

I shrugged. "How the hell would I know? I've never heard her speak. I have a picture, but that's it." I could hear the frustration in my voice.

They shuffled their feet and looked at each other. I stared off for a second, but I couldn't help but recall what I'd heard.

"Dad, I've been waiting to see you. I've always wanted to meet you."

I replayed it over and over again in my head, as the image of Mackenzie's face stuck in my mind.

"What is it? You're thinking something." Alex ran her hand across her head. She had dirty-blond hair, pulled tightly into a ponytail.

"I don't know. Maybe there was something about the girl's voice that sounded a little like her mother's. A little raspy, maybe. I'm not sure. I could just be wanting it to be her. I mean, what do we really know? What proof do we really have that they even have her?"

Nick pressed his thin lips together and offered a short nod.

"Look, I've already sent the voice file up to Gretchen," Alex said. "Nick sent her the pictures of these two goons. She and I spoke a few minutes ago. She's going to start identifying the digital footprint of this entire operation. She just got the video card from Brad, and she's begun to break down the footage into chunks. She said she might have a partial face shot, which she can run through her face-recognition program. You never know, we might get lucky."

I was glad to hear that this Gretchen person was working the hell out of the technology angle. In my lawyer days, that could usually prove, or disprove, any number of theories. But I'd also seen such a reliance on technology that at times it seemed like the cops almost abandoned the most fundamental investigative tactics. Now, though, wasn't the time to get into it.

I released a sigh but winced from another stab of pain in my ribs.

"That's it. You have no choice," Alex said.

A moment later, a guy named Anthony was saying a lot of "oohs" as he examined my torso.

"What's next?" I said, interrupting Alex and Nick in a quiet conversation.

"Don't know yet. Hoping we can get confirmation on these two bozos. That might lead us right to who's holding Mackenzie."

"Then I'm guessing that it will lead nowhere. This group has covered their tracks the whole time. They're one step ahead of us. Actually more like ten steps ahead of us."

Anthony began to clean blood from the cut on the bridge of my nose. "That hurts." I saw Alex and Nick begin to walk away. "Guys, I'm still here. I need to do something. I can't just wait."

Alex backtracked a couple of steps. "Just sit tight for now. We're going to get the team on a call, brainstorm a little bit. Jerry, my boss, is involved now. I've got the full resources of the FBI at my disposal."

Her eyes snagged my gaze. We both nodded, and they walked off. I closed my eyes for a moment, trying to clear my mind.

"Hey, man, can you believe a phone is ringing on the dead man?"

I opened my eyes to see Anthony with a smirk on his face.

"I mean, who's calling a dead guy? Ghostbusters?" He let loose a baritone laugh.

I looked to Mickey, still slouched against the far wall, a sheet of some kind now covering him. The kitchen was temporarily empty, except for Anthony and me.

Anthony persisted. "Can you believe it?" Again with the laugh.

I pushed his hand off my nose, rushed to the dead body, and waited.

A couple of seconds later, I heard a ringing phone from somewhere on Mickey.

A quick glance over my shoulder. No one besides Anthony was looking at me. I pulled back the sheet, fished through Mickey's front pockets, and found a small phone. Didn't recognize the brand. I looked at the number. *Unknown.* I tapped the green button to answer the call but didn't say anything.

"Ozzie, is that you?"

It was a woman. No real accent that I could pick up.

"Yes. Who is this?"

"My name is not important right now. But we will meet in due time."

"Do you have Mackenzie?"

A pause. "Yes, Mackenzie is here with us."

I could feel flames of anger tickling the back of my throat. "Have you hurt her? Is she…" I couldn't say it.

"She is safe. She is surrounded by people who care for her."

"Did you kill Denise?"

"It's not appropriate to go through an interrogation on why certain decisions were made. It was in the best interest of…"

I didn't hear the last word; the phone had cut out. I looked at the screen to make sure the line was still live. It was. "Hello?"

"Ozzie, you have one final leg of this examination. And then you will—"

"I don't believe you."

She didn't respond. I glanced over my shoulder. Anthony, as still as a statue, was staring in my direction.

"What? You can't give up now. It wouldn't be right."

I heard stress in her voice. "You, your group of murderers have done nothing but screw with me for days. What proof do I have that Mackenzie is even with you people?"

"I do not lie."

I choked on my own spit. "You're fucking kidding me, right? That's how you answer? *I do not lie?*"

"We have Mackenzie. She is being taken care of. You heard her recording, did you not? That is real. You can have your FBI friends verify it."

She knew the FBI was involved. It was as if they had a mole on the inside. But unless that mole was Denise—and that, I knew, could not be the case—then there would be no way for them to track my every move. Brook and Stan could have told someone, but they said they hadn't. I believed them. The woman on the line sounded convincing, though. Part of me wanted to believe that Mackenzie was alive. Part of me wanted to tell this woman to go to hell. But despite my skepticism and a torrent of other emotions, I could feel my heart falling for the bait.

"Where is she? What will it take to get her back?" I asked.

"One more test, Ozzie. That's it."

"Stop it with all of your tests and riddles. I want to know where she is."

"Once we end this call, discard your personal phone. You can take this phone—which we will be tracking—while you drive."

"Drive where?"

"Go to Hymie Town. There you must locate the House of Death, where you will find the path to your daughter and everlasting life."

I could feel my lips moving, reciting what she'd just said. Not many people still called New York City "Hymie Town." They must have known I was raised Jewish. And this House of Death... Were they planning on ending this fiasco in some macabre setting? "You'd better not harm Mackenzie."

"Have faith, Ozzie. We do in you."

I was about ready to chuck the phone through the window, but I couldn't lose my temper. If there was even a small chance that Mackenzie was alive, I had to see this through.

"How do I know where in New York City?"

"You have four hours and thirty minutes to arrive at the location. That gives you five minutes to figure that out before you leave. But like I said, do not bring your phone with you in your car. Or we will be forced to..."

I thought I heard a sigh. I ignored it and glanced over my shoulder, looking for the quickest way out.

"Ozzie, two more things. One, you cannot bring your friends from the FBI. If you allow them to track you, again, we will be forced to..."

She didn't want to say it, which, in my instant analysis, seemed odd.

"And the other thing?"

"As it states in Matthew, 'Truly I say to you, that you who have followed Me, in the regeneration when the Son of Man will sit on His glorious throne, you also shall sit upon twelve thrones, judging the twelve tribes of Israel. And everyone who has left houses or brothers or sisters or father or mother or children or farms for My name's sake will receive many times as much, and will inherit eternal life.'"

The line clicked off. I shoved the phone in my front pocket and walked up to Anthony. "You didn't see that, you didn't hear that, okay?"

He just stared at me, eyes wide beneath his furry-caterpillar eyebrows.

"It will be okay, Anthony. Faith." I popped his upper arm and headed through the living room. I could see Alex and Nick in the corner. They both turned in my direction.

"Where you going, Ozzie?"

"Denise gave me an actual print of Mackenzie's picture. It's in the car. I'll be back in a second."

I walked out of the house and through the yard—it appeared even trashier bathed in fake lights. A quick peek over my shoulder. Cops opened and shut the front door, but no one was paying me any attention. And no sign of Alex or Nick.

I traipsed through the brush and made it to my car. I hopped in and jumped on my phone. It was cracked but somehow still functioning. I did a quick search for "House of Death, New York City." I scrolled through a few search results.

"Bingo." I memorized the address, then mapped my route. It seemed rather straightforward, at least getting into New York City, and then from there a few basic turns, so it wasn't difficult to put to memory. I opened my car door and let my phone drop to the pavement.

I knew this could be the most foolish decision I'd ever made.

But if it could save Mackenzie, I'd live with the results.

Forty

Within four miles of driving on State Road, near a town called Wareham, I made a one-eighty-degree loop and merged onto the first of two interstate roads I'd need to take, I-195. It swooped south, skimmed the edge of something called Buzzards Bay, and then gradually began to loop northward. An hour into the trip, I'd yet to see a cop or state trooper.

The act of surprise had probably given me a decent head start on law enforcement. Alex and Nick, their whole team, along with Brook and Stan… I owed them a great deal. They'd agreed to put their lives on hold and assist me in every way possible to navigate this maze of deception. Their unrelenting determination had given me hope when I'd thought I had none. But as much as I appreciated their support, I was given no option by the woman on the phone. I couldn't tell my FBI friends, have them tag along—even at a safe distance—and still have any faith that the kidnappers wouldn't know. Maybe was I wrong in my assessment. Nick, as an example, might say I was giving the kidnappers more credit than they deserved. But up until this point, they'd not only anticipated every move, they'd planned it out as if they were experts in clandestine project management.

The roads were nearly empty, but I made sure to drive at the speed limit. I couldn't afford to zip by a cop at more than eighty miles an hour. Even if he were snoozing in the darkness behind a billboard, he'd probably sense my speeding and then chase me down just for the fun of it. And when he pulled me over, he'd check my identification, then realize that I was a person of interest—or some similar term to ensure it got the attention of officers in the tristate area—in this kidnapping thing. Just the time I'd have to spend negotiating with the officer would ruin my chances of reaching this House of Death within the window given by the mysterious woman on the phone.

I could practically hear the cussing coming out of Alex and Nick, even though they were a hundred miles to my east. They both seemed to be rather intense, especially Alex. She, however, might use the term *focused*.

I started crossing bodies of water—large lakes and rivers. I saw a sign for Brown University as I swept through the south side of Providence. Yes, I was in Rhode Island. It was, apparently, a rather circuitous route to get from Massachusetts to New York City.

My mind began to drift back to my conversation with the woman. Two key points stood out for me. First was her hesitancy to show complete ruthlessness. She didn't want to say that they would be forced to kill Mackenzie. Even thinking it made the veins in my head feel like they might burst, but why would she have an issue with it? Hell, she was the one, or at least part of the group, who had done the kidnapping.

Second, she'd used another Bible verse. I didn't put it to memory, but I recalled phrases such as "you who have followed me," the mentioning of "the twelve tribes of Israel," and, at the very end, something about "inheriting eternal life."

I then recalled the Bible verse Mickey had uttered. This one had stuck with me: *"Whoever seeks to keep his life will lose it, and whoever loses his life will preserve it."*

That seemed to reflect his position at the time—taking some suicide pill and believing that he'd somehow secured some type of preserved life.

Preserved life. Inheriting eternal life. Hmmm.

I wondered if saying these verses was just a ritual for these people or if they held any significant clues as to what they were all about. I knew that religious phrases could be spun to support almost any point of view, and it was usually the crazy people who clung to the ones that incited violence or retribution. I just never understood why the followers of such crazy people—whether it was in a cult, in a so-called "terrorist group," or even through a televangelist—would flock to such nonsense.

I blinked a couple of times, tried to gingerly wipe my eyes so that I wouldn't reopen the cut. I didn't smell or feel blood on my fingers, but the pain level was off the charts. I released a couple of cuss words, smacked my hand against the passenger seat, if for no other reason than to get out some of my rage.

I realized I was now in Connecticut, driving on a part of I-95 that was labeled Jewish War Veterans Memorial Highway.

A coincidence? Who knew?

The interstate morphed into a series of smaller highways, and I finally made it into New York. The closer I got to New York City, my paranoia about being pulled over lessened. I saw signs for Mount Vernon and Yonkers, then slid east onto the Hudson Parkway. I peeked at the Hudson River to my right. It appeared so calm and peaceful. For whatever reason, I pictured that huge jet floating in it, the one from a few years ago when Captain "Sully" had landed the plane under the most extreme, dire circumstances.

He'd kept a steady hand and logically worked through the troubleshooting steps with remarkable poise under pressure.

I took a breath, hoping to channel some of Sully's cool composure.

Off to my left, the bright lights and countless tall buildings of Manhattan were almost mind-numbing. I'd been to New York City only once, back when I was in law school at Georgetown and came up this way with some friends. I had been a bit enamored back then. Now, the labyrinth of streets and alleys and tall buildings just made it seem like Mackenzie was the needle in the city haystack.

I finally turned east on West 14th. Throughout the entire trip, I'd tried not to obsess over the reasoning behind sending me to this House of Death. My palms started to sweat. Now, all sorts of crazy ideas bounced around my mind, some even involving ghosts. The combination of no sleep and the repeated surges of adrenaline had left me weary. The kind where you feel it in your bones.

After I turned south on 7th Avenue, I picked up the phone I'd taken off Mickey and wondered if it might ring. Of course, it didn't, so I put it back on the seat. I was about a mile away from the destination. Was this House of Death their actual headquarters? Their way of hiding in plain sight?

I came onto West 10th, slowed down, took in everything around me. Outside of a mattress store and a couple other businesses, it was all row homes made of red brick, with most of the front doors a few steps below street level. Trees dotted the sidewalks, apparently an attempt to break up the mass of concrete.

This was no Austin.

Ten minutes prior to my deadline, I pulled to a stop in front of 14 West 10th. Ivy was draped over a second-floor plant box. All the windows were covered. There was an awning over the entrance, and a single light was on next to the front door. I glanced around. No pedestrians in the immediate vicinity.

This had to be a trap, right? I mean, up until now, this group had been playing to my worst fears, using both the carrot and the stick to prod me into taking that next step.

Mickey's phone rang, and I jumped in my seat. So much for the act of channeling Sully.

"Hello," I said.

"I'm glad you made it. I can't tell you how relieved we are."

The same woman again. She sounded like a relative, maybe an aunt, sharing her happiness that I'd safely arrived. But I wasn't stupid. There was more to my arrival than picking up Mackenzie and just driving off. Part of me wished Alex and Nick were a block away, waiting to raid this place and finally end this nightmare. We'd save Mackenzie, and the two of us would begin our lives together.

Had I fucked this up?

"Okay. Where is Mackenzie?"

"We left a light on for you. As I noted, you must follow the path. I'm only calling because I know the house can appear to be a bit…morbid."

I wouldn't have used that term. But she had. So, either something had gone down at this home or their interior decorator was from another world.

With the phone still at my ear, I slipped out of the Buick, walked onto the sidewalk, and looked around. The street was empty. All clear. I wasn't sure if that was good news.

"Are you still there, Ozzie?"

Her voice sounded like she was the receptionist at a spa. Too serene for this situation.

"Yes." I stared at the front door.

"Come on in. You'll be warmly received."

"Bring Mackenzie outside."

A pause. "You know we can't do that."

"Why not?"

"We know that you have never met your daughter. I'm sure it will be an emotional experience for both of you. Plus, given our situation, we'd rather handle the hand-over in a quieter setting. I'm sure you understand."

"I don't understand shit." I anchored my feet to the concrete. Defiant.

The woman sighed into the phone. "I hate to remind you, but technically you have not arrived at the destination. You have two minutes until time runs out."

A burst of emotion sent tears into my eyes. The emotion was partly seething anger, partly fright for losing Mackenzie.

"Okay, okay," I said, gritting my teeth.

I went down the steps, put my hand on the doorknob, and turned it. Not surprisingly, it was unlocked. I walked into a small foyer. There was a nightlight glowing under a table against the wall. I walked over and picked up one of those things girls used to pull their hair back. This one was rainbow-colored.

"Where is—"

A stabbing jolt in my side before I could finish my question. My whole body buzzed like I'd touched a live electric wire, and I dropped to the floor. No control of my muscles. Nothing. Shoes shuffled around me. A rag was jammed into my mouth. It smelled sweet, like honey, but I knew it had to be chloroform. I clenched my muscles, trying with everything in my power to fight back. It was as if the signal had been cut from my brain. Two short breaths, and my eyes shut.

My last coherent thought was wondering if the rainbow-colored hair tie belonged to Mackenzie.

Forty-One

$$\text{---------}\bowtie\bowtie\bowtie\text{---------}$$

A shove, maybe two, and then yanking at my wrists and ankles. Seconds passed, maybe a minute. I could have fallen back asleep. Eventually, I peeled my eyes open and took in a faint breath. My vision, all of my senses, were off. Well, I knew my hearing was off, but nothing else seemed normal, either.

I was alone in the darkness. A chill coursed through my body. My muscles responded but only slightly. I had no real strength.

"Mackenzie," I said, barely able to push out a sound.

No response. No movement.

I tried clearing my throat, but it was like moving a mountain. It wasn't going to happen. Lifting my head, my mind gained just a tad more clarity. My ankles and wrists were tied to something. I was on my butt, and my back was pressed against a metal wall, which was not smooth.

I blinked, and a door swung open, breaking the darkness. *Ah, so, I'm in a van.* Two men got in, speaking so fast I couldn't understand them. One of them laughed. I looked down. I had no clothes on. Still, laughter or not, embarrassment wasn't a concern for me.

"Where's Mackenzie?" I said as my head rocked left and right, with no real control.

One of them grunted, moved in closer. He had a lot of missing teeth. One-liners started shooting into my mind, but I was in a fight for my life. For Mackenzie's life. At least I hoped I was.

A cold object against my side.

"Don't. Don't, please."

They didn't care. Mr. Jack-o-lantern zapped me with the taser, and my entire body locked up. It was as if I'd been turned into stone. They weren't done. A wet rag was stuffed into my mouth. I last recalled seeing the door shut and then feeling the sudden thrust of the van taking off.

Once again, my eyes shut, and darkness prevailed.

Forty-Two

"**W**ake up. Wake up, Ozzie."

A voice from another world.

Hands were on me, grabbing at my shirt. My body was jostled. *I have a shirt on?*

"What, what, what…?" A breath exploded from my chest as my eyes shot open. "Where am I?" I reached out a hand and felt metal. It was coarse.

"Ozzie, it's me."

I blinked, turned my head. A young girl was pulling at my sweatshirt. It was dark wherever we were, but I could still see dirt caked onto her face, sprinkled in her hair.

"Mackenzie?" I gently touched her upper arm.

She nodded. "I've been waiting on you. Everyone's been waiting on you."

She did sound like her mother. But she looked like…me.

"How...?" I turned away, looking out through a metal cage. I touched it—rebar. People shuffled by in worn boots and work clothes. I saw one head turn in my direction. He was serious looking, but I thought I noticed a smile play at the corners of his mouth.

It was daytime, though the sky was gray. A blanket of fog nipped at the tops of tall trees. We were in the middle of a forest.

Back to Mackenzie. I held her arms. "Have they harmed you?"

"No. Not really. Some of them have been mean. They've kept me in this pen."

We were sitting down. The pen was no more than four feet tall, maybe six feet wide, six feet deep.

"It gets cold, especially at night." She reached behind her and grabbed something that looked like it had been buried underground. "I have this blanket."

They'd been forcing her to live in squalor. I could feel my blood rippling through my veins. But at least I felt something. I ran my hands across the rebar outlining this mini-prison cell. It seemed to be put together well. A chain wrapped through the tiny door, secured by a keyed padlock.

"How long have I been here?"

"A couple of hours, I think. They've already had their lunch."

"What have you been doing while I've just been sitting here knocked out?"

She shrugged her shoulders, her eyes finding the ground.

I touched her chin. "Mackenzie, you can tell me anything."

She swallowed, then swept some of her frizzy hair away from her face. "I've been leaning against your shoulder."

"That's okay. I'm glad you did." A warm sensation filled my core. I started to bring her in for a hug when she said...

"I know Mom is dead." Tears leaped out of her blue eyes, and she buried her face against my shoulder.

I wrapped my arm around her and let her cry for a moment. I bit into the side of my cheek to keep my emotions at bay. I whispered, "I'm so sorry, Mackenzie."

Her sobs grew deeper, and she began to pull on my sweatshirt. I held on to her, wishing I could make the pain go away. A week or so ago, I was wallowing in the aftermath of what I'd considered a torturous experience, trying to figure out a way to deal with all the betrayal and resentment and outright viciousness. And now, here I was, holding my child—yes, my own flesh and blood—as she mourned the death of her mother. I thought then of the video. Mackenzie could never know what had happened to her mother.

"Your mom loved you with all her heart." I kissed the top of her head. She put her arms around my torso and squeezed. My ribs felt a stab, but the pain meant nothing. She could hold on to me for hours if it would help her get through this torment.

A clapping noise drew my attention outside the pen. I saw the legs of four people. Then a face appeared just on the other side of the rebar. It was long and thin, with an egg-shaped mouth, like one of those Halloween masks.

"What a pleasure it is to finally meet the great Ozzie Novak." He clapped and chuckled. "I'm Joseph. Welcome to my Kingdom."

Forty-Three

"I hope you're comfortable," he said, still smiling, looking around our pen as if he were a hotel manager checking on a penthouse suite.

Mackenzie slinked behind my shoulder. It seemed as though she were hiding from Joseph, leader of this…kingdom.

"Why do you have us locked up?"

"Because you're our guest." He glanced up at the three people standing by him, and they grunted acknowledgement. I couldn't see their faces. "Guests are not members," he said, holding up a finger as if he were teaching me a lesson meant for a four-year-old. I was so tempted to reach between the gaps in the rebar and snatch his finger. I wouldn't just break it; I'd hold on until I snapped it off.

"But I hope you know how special you are to us," he said, bobbing his head up and down. He had wavy hair and an accent that said he was more farmer than charismatic leader.

"Special," I muttered.

He continued to nod. "I hope you know we meant no one harm. But the time has come," he said, shaking that finger again. "This world cannot continue down its current path. No, it just can't. We must initiate the necessary change to enable the flock to follow us down a righteous path. All sinners will be gone. Mark my word."

I could feel my forehead fold, which gave me the sensation of a knife slicing my skin.

"I can see you have doubt." He moved his robe behind his back and raised his arms as if he were signaling a touchdown. "The good Lord knows all, and through his closest living prophet, He has chosen me to be His surrogate to the people of this land," he said, now patting his chest.

This guy seemed as believable as a carnival employee. Why was I the only one who could see it?

"Why are you keeping us here?" I asked with more force than I'd intended. "And when will you let us go?"

"Go," he said, nodding. He looked at the people above his head. Then he set his eyes back on me. He squinted, studying me. "You have no idea how long I've looked forward to this day."

I wanted to say, *"Well, I'm here, ass wipe. Open up this cage and let's go a couple of rounds."* Instead, I said in my calmest voice, "Why am I so important to you, this kingdom?"

He pursed his lips. "As Malachi once said, 'Fix our eyes not on what is seen, but on what is unseen, since what is seen is temporary, but what is unseen is eternal."

Well, isn't that grand?

"Your time has come, Ozzie." He looked me straight in the eye, then he fell back into carny mode. "There is a time for everything, and a season for every activity under the heavens." He paused. "Stick out your arm."

"What? Why?" I scooted back a few inches, Mackenzie still behind me.

He snapped his fingers. "Do you not sip the wine before you drink from the bottle?"

I had no clue what he was talking about. Hesitantly, I stuck my hand through the rebar. Two men dropped to their knees and grabbed my arm. Instinctively, I pulled back. But they were big and strong. I recognized one of the brawny guys from the van.

I struggled against their sizable weight advantage, but in my reduced strength, I was at their mercy. Suddenly, the guy from the van pulled out a knife and held it skyward. Then Joseph did some type of ritual crossing over it and kissed it. Yes, he kissed the blade of a frickin' knife. In a split second, they opened my hand and sliced a wedge right down the middle.

"No!" Mackenzie yelled.

They turned my hand, pumped on my arm, and forced the blood to drip into a cup. They let go, and I fell back into Mackenzie. A dirty rag was thrown into the pen.

Joseph leaned over. "Tonight as the moon rises and sun sets, the chosen one will drinketh from the chalice the sacred blood, the one who will fill him with the essence of Malachi."

He flapped his cape as if he were Batman and then marched away followed by his two-goon squad.

"Ozzie, are you okay?" Mackenzie took the rag and tried to mop up blood from the cut. "Tell me you're not going to die." I could hear panic in her voice.

"It will be okay, Mackenzie. I'm here for you. I'm not going anywhere."

I could feel eyes on us. I flipped to look over my shoulder. It was a woman. She had long, flat hair. She wore no makeup, and her skin was pasty white.

"I can see that she already cares for you like a daughter would her father."

It was the woman from the phone. Had to be. I studied her for a second, and she did the same of me. She shifted her sights to

Mackenzie. A single tear escaped her eye. She quickly wiped it away. "I'm sorry, but this has to be."

And then she was gone.

Forty-Four

The pounding of the drums started at sunset and didn't stop. They grew louder over time. Mackenzie huddled at my side, neither of us speaking much. Our eyes were unblinking, staring out from the pen, trying to see the location of the campsite where sacrifices were made on an almost nightly basis. Earlier, Mackenzie had shared that interesting bit of intel with me. With a tear in her eye, she'd told me that she could hear the squeal of animals as they burned to death over a fire.

I didn't want to tell her that many of the foods she'd eaten came from animals who'd died in inhumane ways. It didn't matter. Seeing her compassion for other living things had shown me another side to my daughter.

My daughter.

I couldn't let Mackenzie die. We'd been together for mere hours, but the connection I felt inside was unlike anything I'd experienced in my life. It was real and undeniable.

I'd been racking my brain all afternoon, trying to understand the psyche of the players involved, searching for any type of hole that might ultimately allow us to live or, better yet, to be free. This Joseph guy was a real piece of shit. He'd somehow convinced these poor souls to believe his garbage. But for what? To lead the world down a new path of righteousness? Back in Austin, I'd hear crackpots like that every other week on some street corner. Mostly, they were ignored. Sometimes people would drop a buck or two into their "donation bins" just because they felt sorry for a person who'd obviously gone off the rails.

But was that Joseph's actual goal—to lead this group like he was Moses?

I glanced down and saw the blood-soaked rag wrapped around my hand, and my mind, now finally working on all cylinders, started dissecting everything that Joseph had said.

"The good Lord knows all, and through his closest living prophet, he has chosen me to be his surrogate to the people of this land."

Through his closest living prophet.

When he'd first said it, the phrase had gotten lost in all the other nonsensical gibberish. Was the "closest living prophet" real? An actual person guiding Joseph? I'd seen Joseph exit out of some primitive-looking building at the far end of the camp. I wondered if he had a computer in there, how he might be communicating with this "living prophet."

Mackenzie moved behind me and started drawing in the dirt. I could see it was her way of escaping this craziness. A sense of dread hung over us like a fog blanket. Any words of encouragement from me would surely be met with a roll of the eyes, if not a more irate response. She was a young girl who'd experienced something I could never have fathomed at nine years of age. I was too busy playing ball outside, swimming, or battling my brother for video-game dominance.

She swept some of her curly hair out of her face and focused on the vignette she was creating, giving me a moment to reorient my thoughts on Joseph's ramblings. He was a big believer in the Old Testament, quoting from the book of Malachi twice.

"As Malachi has once said, 'Fix our eyes not on what is seen, but on what is unseen, since what is seen is temporary, but what is unseen is eternal.'"

My mind went to the word "eternal."

"Tonight as the moon rises and sun sets, the chosen one will drinketh from the chalice the sacred blood, the one who will fill him with the essence of Malachi."

Damn, he was talking about my blood.

I wasn't stupid, and I doubted that they'd brought me across the country to "sip the wine."

Without openly saying it, I was their sacrifice to roast over a fire like a skewered pig. *"Your time has come, Ozzie."*

I took in a breath and tried to keep my anger from getting the best of me. I wrapped the fingers from my good hand around the rebar and squeezed until it hurt. Rattling the cage, throwing a fit, would only draw more attention to us. If anything, we needed the opposite. More time, less attention.

I began to mimic Mackenzie, running my pointer finger through the dirt, allowing all the information I'd heard, all the horror I'd witnessed over the last several days to soak in the same mental bucket.

It came to me in mere seconds, as if my brain had just found the secret door to a treasure. I remembered sitting in the TGI Friday's in LAX and Denise reading to me the story of Camp Israel, of the people who'd been held captive for thirty years. The leader of that group—Malachi.

I wasn't sure why I'd blocked this piece of data from my mind.

Now, I recounted Joseph's words with a filter in a place. And I asked myself one question: was there any way the "closest living prophet" was none other than Malachi? He was in prison, or so Alex and Nick had been led to believe. That had been one of their tasks, to see if he was still behind bars.

What if he wasn't? What if he'd escaped and was the true leader of this cult?

Mackenzie turned and looked at me, trying to smile. I put my hand against her face, and she leaned into it. Then her eyes went wide. "Look, it's Cecelia."

It took me a second to see through a number of people walking by us, likely headed to the festivities down by the ring of fire— wasn't that a Johnny Cash song? Anyway, I followed her gaze until I found the woman who'd been here earlier, the one from the phone, leaning against the building, her hands in her pockets. She looked off in the distance and then back to us. Then again, the same routine.

"Her name is Cecelia?" I asked, my eyes still on the woman.

"That's what I heard Joseph call her. He used her name a lot that one night when he got into the pen with me."

I flipped my head around. "Do what? Did he...?"

"Stranger danger. My mom told me all about it. No way that guy was going to touch me, not in that way. I kicked and scratched and did everything to keep him off me. Finally, he gave up and said something about having his way with Cecelia. Since then, he's stayed away." She paused as her eyes looked beyond me.

"What do you want from us?"

I turned to see Cecelia at the cage.

Forty-Five

———◦◦◦———

Cecelia wrapped her fingers around the rebar. It almost seemed as though she wanted to be inside the pen with us. And there, I saw a crack I could exploit.

"Do you like it here in this camp, Cecelia?"

She shifted her eyes to me and blinked. She looked tired. "What do you mean?"

"Joseph and all his rituals and sacrifices. Is this really who you are?"

She swallowed and blinked again. "He means well. We're following the prophet. Through his guidance, we can change the course of the world."

"Is this prophet named Malachi?"

She didn't respond.

"I know about Camp Israel, remember? You guys sent me there."

Mackenzie leaned against me. No way I was going to bring up the death of her mom.

"We did our research. He's the prophet, isn't he? That's who's giving Joseph this edict to change the world."

She turned her head, looking away from us.

"Do you know the story of Malachi? By the way, I think his real name is Eldridge Kaufman."

"Yes, I read about it. But Joseph has a deeper connection, both with the Lord and the prophet. He knows him in a different way."

"Do you know what he did to people? Do you know that, behind everyone's back, he was simply trying to scam innocent people out of their money?"

She wiped her face and scanned the ground.

"What? Please tell me what you're thinking, Cecelia. Because here in a few minutes, your people, led by Joseph, might be roasting me over a fire." I'd purposely kept Mackenzie out of the conversation, but I was almost certain they would not allow her to live.

The crowd behind Cecelia was thinning out, which meant that most people were probably gathered by the fire pit. She brought her hand to her lips, as if she were trying to keep words locked inside.

"Cecelia. I can see you're a good person. Even the way you spoke to me over the phone. You're not like Joseph." I paused, waiting for a response, even a signal. Nothing came. "None of us are perfect, Cecelia. We're human. We've made mistakes, but it's not too late to change. I'm just like you. I've made tons of mistakes in my life. And I'm sure I'll make—"

"It's you, okay?" she blurted out, jerking her head to me.

"Me? What about me?"

She picked up a handful of dirt, then tossed it back to the ground. "Ozzie, your blood is Malachi's blood."

I suddenly became lightheaded. My hands balled into fists, my nails digging into the cut on my one hand. I breathed out the word, "What?"

"You, Ozzie, are Malachi's son. This is why Joseph wants to make you a sacrifice, to drink your blood. He believes he's channeling Malachi by drinking the blood of his son."

If I'd been standing, I might have keeled over. As it was, my heart couldn't beat any faster.

"Ozzie, what is she saying?" Mackenzie asked, pulling at my sweatshirt.

I patted my daughter on her head, and she rested it against my shoulder. She seemed to sense that her questions could wait until later. I trained my eyes on Cecelia, sizing her up. Was this another one of their ninja mind tricks? She didn't look away. Our stare-off lasted a good thirty seconds.

"I'm adopted," I said.

"I know. We know everything about your life, Ozzie."

Something thumped my chest. The drums, my heart…I couldn't tell for sure.

"You passed all the tests. You have his unbreakable will. You are just like—"

"Don't say it." Now I was the one looking away. A murdering sociopath? I'm his son? How?

I tried to speak, but I couldn't formulate a coherent thought.

"You were going to find out before…" she said, her words trailing off.

"How do you know this is true?"

"We have people in places. They want to be part of this global change. It means something to them."

"Like Gwen?"

Cecelia's chest hitched just a bit, but she didn't confirm it.

"I wondered if she had somehow been wrapped up in this." I glanced down at Mackenzie, still leaning against me. She was playing with a few strands of hair, seemingly in another world. I looked back at Cecelia. Part of me wanted to just rip her a new one, for the deception, the kidnapping of an innocent child, the assaults, killing Denise, possibly killing others as well. And for what? To see if I could stand up to some bizarre set of tests to prove I was worthy of them sacrificing me, drinking my blood?

"You don't approve—I understand. Many have sacrificed to get us where we are today. But after tonight, we begin the pilgrimage."

"To where? To do what? This is nuts, Cecelia. Killing anyone…drinking blood won't change the world. It takes sensible people sitting down and connecting, finding common ground. It takes respect. Not killing. Not deceiving."

She didn't argue the point.

Mackenzie sat up, lifted my arm, and put her head on my lap. Cecelia's eyes lingered on my daughter.

"Just know that you are a lucky man to finally see your daughter before, you know…" Her eyes became glassy.

I sensed she'd experienced loss. Another possible opening. And I knew I had only one more shot.

"She's a gift," I said in a calm tone, nodding.

She didn't move her sights off Mackenzie, but there was something behind her eyes that told me more.

"Cecelia, did you lose a daughter?"

She went still, her eyes dazed.

"I didn't mean to—"

"I was a rebel when I was young. Always partying, looking to mingle with the older crowd. This charming guy, Drew Stanley, caught my eye. He said I caught his, but I now know the truth." Tears welled, but that didn't stop her. "I got pregnant. I was only fifteen. Drew wanted no part of me or the baby. He spit in my face when I told him."

She paused. In a normal setting, I might have reached out, touched her arm. But the rebar cage and the situation prevented that response.

"We lived in a small town in rural Indiana. No way would I be able to have a kid out of wedlock, not at that age. My parents sent me off to my aunt's home in Los Angeles, where I put the baby up for adoption."

Tears rolled down her face. She wiped one away but stopped after that.

"You miss her, don't you?"

She looked down, nodded.

"It's not too late, Cecelia. There are ways to find your kids. I'm a lawyer. I can help you. I have friends who can help you."

She squeezed her eyes shut. "But I don't deserve her. I gave her away."

"You can't blame yourself for something that happened when you were fifteen. But it really doesn't matter what age you were. We make decisions every day that can be ridiculed at any point in the future. It's part of being human."

She looked up at me, hope in her eyes.

"The point is, you miss her. And that makes complete sense. I have a feeling that, if you reached out, she'll want to get to know her mom. Her real mom."

She bit into her bottom lip, eyes darting everywhere, finally landing on Mackenzie.

Some type of horn blew off in the distance.

"I've got to go and get ready." She wiped her face, pulled a cross necklace out from under her shirt, leaned over, and said a quick prayer.

"Cecelia, we can help each other."

She got to her knees, glanced at me briefly, and then pushed up and walked away.

"Cecelia." I put my face against the rebar as I watched our only hope walk off.

We were all alone. Although I knew, in a few minutes, the goon squad would come back to get us and take us to our deaths.

I grabbed the rebar with both hands and shook it with everything I had. It hardly budged.

"Ozzie," Mackenzie said.

"What?" I asked, with my face now pressed against the rebar, catching the last glimpse of Cecelia fading into the horde of people. Then I saw a flame flicker to life.

They'd started the fire.

"Ozzie, look at what I found."

Mackenzie got in front of me and held a key in front of my face.

"Where did you find this?"

"On the ground, right by the edge of the cage," she said, patting the dirt.

Cecelia had left it for us, I was certain. I quickly tried the key in the padlock. It fit. I turned the key, unhooked the lock from the chain, and slowly scooted the door open about a foot. I pushed Mackenzie through the small opening, then wedged myself out while keeping one eye on the group by the growing fire. They were all chanting something.

We got to our feet, and she took my hand. There was a path into the woods, and we ran like our feet were on fire.

Forty-Six

—————

My legs felt like they weren't mine, so Mackenzie and I ran at about the same pace. I took a quick peek down at her. She was pumping her arms, her cheeks puffing out with each breath. Damn, I was proud of her grit, her unyielding desire to cling to life in the prison, and now this brave push to get out of this hellhole.

The woods were thick, and while a little glare from above helped to see the ground, I had to just pray that we wouldn't trip over anything—that was the main reason I kept us on the path.

"Do you think...do you think...we're safe?" Mackenzie asked, barely able to get words out through her stressed lungs.

"Don't know. Let's keep going."

Not more than a few steps later, she stopped on a dime. I pulled up. "We need to go. Come on."

She brought a finger up to her mouth. "Shh."

I glanced around. Nothing was moving, but I couldn't hear if anyone might be lurking behind a tree.

I asked, "What do you hear?"

"Nothing." I tried grabbing her hand. She pulled it away and said, "I was hearing the drums while we were running. They were really low, but I heard them. Now I don't."

"Maybe we're finally too far." I reached for her hand again.

She shook her head. I twisted around, scanning the area with eyes that I wished had night-vision. As I moved back a step, I saw glint of light through the cracks of the wilderness.

I pointed in that direction. "Shit. That's the camp. I think we might have circled back on this path. Fuck! Come on."

She said something, but I didn't hear her. I took her hand and headed off the path, moving directly away from the campsite. Our pace had been cut in half—we couldn't see a damn thing until it was on top of us—but it was worth it to put real distance between us and the nutjobs.

Another minute passed, and then I saw a clearing. "Let's pick it up." I began to jog, and Mackenzie fell in right behind me. The cold air singed my lungs, but in some respects, it felt good. I was doing something to keep us alive, which beat the hell out of helplessly walking to the fire pit and being burned alive.

I cut around a tree and began to see white on some of the limbs. It had been snowing. We might freeze out in the middle of... Where were we? Not only did I not know what direction we were running, I had no clue what city or state we were in.

"You're doing awesome, Mackenzie," I said.

"Thanks." She had some pep in her voice. She seemed to like the positive reinforcement. I could sense that she felt the same hope that I did.

"We're making progress. Another five minutes or so, and then we'll—"

I felt the pop in my hip at the exact moment my shoe jammed into something hard. My head dipped forward. My momentum sent me airborne. The next thing I knew, my face slammed into the frozen dirt.

I moaned. "Mackenzie?" I looked up, didn't see her. Hearing what sounded like a chuckle, I flipped around. A tall silhouette was holding Mackenzie, who was trying to shake her way loose.

I got up on all fours, ready to lunge at the guy.

"Don't make a move."

A light flicked on. It was the glow of his phone moving up next to his ear—the guy from the van was smiling as he waited for whomever to pick up the line. I could just make out Mackenzie's face. He had his arm hooked around her body, the barrel of a pistol pressed into her chin.

"Stop moving," I yelled to Mackenzie. She froze.

"Found 'em. Yep. Up here, just forty yards south of the north 2A zone. Right. Out." He pressed a button, turned on his flashlight, and shined it in my face. I turned my head for a second.

"You have sinned, Ozzie. Tsk, tsk, tsk."

"Why are you doing this?" I asked, not expecting a good reason. "Look. Just let us go, and we'll make sure the authorities know you helped us. They'll let you off."

"You think I'm some kind of ignoramus country boy?"

He'd asked, but I refused to say what I was thinking. "You're the smartest one of the whole bunch." Damn, I needed his name to really connect. "And smart people make the best decisions under stress. You don't want to go to prison, do you?"

He brought the phone to his chin and scratched it.

I looked over my shoulder. I could see a bouncing light moving our way. Back to the guy. I said, "Come on. Let us go, and you're safe."

"I wouldn't let you go if Jesus dropped down on this Earth and did a dance in a silly little dress right in front of me." He snorted out a laugh.

Something moved in the darkness behind him. His head bobbed forward slightly.

"Drop the gun before I put a bullet through your skull."

"Alex?"

The man dropped his gun as Alex wheeled around to where I could see her. She was the most beautiful thing I'd ever seen…aside from my little girl. "Hey there," she said, her eyes and gun still trained on the stupid sap.

Mackenzie rammed into my chest just then. She hugged me and began to cry.

"Get down on your knees," Alex said to the man.

"I'm not doing anything a woman tells me to do, no matter what you have in your hands."

Quicker than I could say *Mackenzie*, Alex had snapped her arm and popped the guy on the nose with the butt of her pistol. He dropped to his knees, squealing like a pig. His phone also dropped, and the light from the screen shined upward. Alex asked me to pick up the man's gun. The moment I had the gun in my hand, I heard another voice.

"Everyone just needs to stay calm and not move a muscle."

I turned to see two dark figures. It sounded like Joseph, but someone was in front of him.

I said, "It's over, Joseph. The FBI is here and—"

"Alex Troutt, I believe."

A pause.

"That's me. Why don't you come over and shake my hand," she said. I could see her gun aimed in the direction of Joseph.

How did he know Alex? It must have been her connection to Camp Israel and that lunatic who ran it, Malachi. He was my father. I would have hurled from the thought had I not been worried about surviving this situation.

"While I didn't predict it, I knew it was a possibility, given your skill set and history." Joseph sounded a little too happy right now.

I began to hear whimpers as the person in front of him moved, grunting something indecipherable.

Then I heard, "I don't want to die."

My heartbeat skipped. "Cecelia?"

"I now know that she gave you the key, Ozzie," Joseph said, his voice commanding obedience. "And that's too bad. I was growing fond of her. But sometimes it takes a village, if you know what I mean."

I didn't, which I was certain was a good thing. "Joseph, just let her go. She actually wants to have a normal life. She wants to see her daughter."

He started laughing. "Everyone seems so attached to their family." He paused, then said, "But what about the work of Malachi? He had this vision, and so help me God, we will carry it out. All you sinners will go to hell as a result of impeding his plans. *My plans*." The roar of his voice practically shook the trees.

The guy on the ground moved, which jostled the light. I could now see Joseph holding a foot-long knife to Cecelia's throat.

He said to his follower, "Get her gun. And he has one too."

The man got to his feet, grabbed the gun out of my hand. I made sure Mackenzie was right at my side. He took two steps toward Alex. "Hand it over."

"No way," she said.

Joseph laughed. "If you want this piece of trash to live, then you'll drop it."

She reset her feet, chin up, challenging.

"Did you hear me, Alex? I will kill her, with the blessing of the great prophet. I can hear him speaking to me right now, so help me God."

"Let her go first," she said.

"We're not going to play chicken. You drop it, or she dies."

Alex looked in my direction and let the gun fall to the ground.

"Good girl." I saw the white of Joseph's teeth, then watched his lips as he said, "And sinners will never be allowed to join the Kingdom."

"No!" I yelled. Before I got the words out, Joseph had sliced Cecelia's neck. She stumbled, reaching for the wound, and fell.

Mackenzie buried her face in my side. "No, no, no," she said.

"You're nothing but a lowlife piece of shit," Alex said, pointing a finger at him.

I could hear the other guy laughing and snorting.

Joseph said, "We're all just having fun, right? Now, let's get on back to camp. I think we just hit the jackpot on sacrifices. Oh my, Malachi will be ecstatic to hear how this turned out."

Two quick pings, and the minion's face exploded.

"Get down." Alex jumped on Mackenzie.

I saw Joseph spin around and run. Despite my hip not feeling right, I chased him down in about four strides and threw him to the ground.

"It's Nick," I heard Alex say.

"Come get this asshole," I said, flipping around to look over my shoulder. Nick was heading in my direction. He jogged within ten feet, then yelled, "Move!" I flinched, moved, and he fired the gun.

The bullet whizzed past my ear and connected with Joseph, who had another knife in his hand. He fell straight back.

"Dude, you almost gave me a heart attack," I said, jumping to my feet as Nick patted me on the back. "Mackenzie?" I found her in the haze of light. She ran right for me and jumped into my arms.

For a brief moment, all was right in the world.

Forty-Seven

———————

"**W**here are we?" I asked Alex as about three dozen SWAT, police, and FBI agents roamed through the camp known as Kingdom. Mackenzie had a blanket wrapped around her. We were sitting at a picnic table. She'd been like Velcro on me since the final kill shot.

"About twenty miles north of the Allenwood Federal Prison."

"Isn't that in Pennsylvania?"

"Yep," Nick said, pacing next to us.

"How did you find us?"

Alex said, "I told you I had a great team. We learned that Eldridge had been transferred from a prison in Kansas to the Allenwood prison six months ago."

"But how did you know I was here?"

"We weren't a hundred percent sure. Thanks for trying to elude us, though." She gave me a faux smile.

"Sorry, but I really thought I had no choice."

"I know. I figured something else might go down, which is why I slipped a GPS chip into your back pocket in the kitchen back in Plymouth."

"Seriously? Nice trusting relationship we have."

"We had each other's backs, right?"

I grinned. "But wait—they took off all my clothes once I got into New York City."

"We were two blocks away. We tracked the van as far as we could go without being seen. We got to within about twenty miles of this place. And then we worked with local officials to figure out the best places for a campsite. The rest is history."

"I owe you everything, Alex." I put my arm around Mackenzie. "We both do."

She looked at Mackenzie. "I got two at home just like her. They're the most imperfect jewels you'll ever own."

"Imperfect?" I said, slightly taken aback. "What do you mean?"

She smiled. "Just wait until they become teenagers. You'll get it."

Forty-Eight

$\longrightarrow$ ⊂⊘⊘⊘⊐ $\longrightarrow$

Mackenzie and I were whisked away to Harrisburg, about a ninety-minute drive south of the camp location, and set up in an actual hotel. With room service, Mackenzie noticed once we'd arrived.

"You use that as much as you want," Alex told her.

"I would love some pizza." Mackenzie went over to the phone, but held up before dialing. She looked at me for approval. It seemed strange to me, but I tried to act as normal as possible. "You heard Alex; it's okay. Plus, the FBI is paying for it. Right, Alex?"

Alex smiled and then winked at Mackenzie.

We spent three more days in Pennsylvania. Mackenzie watched countless episodes of *Young Justice* and *Girl Meets World*. Occasionally, we'd be interrupted by Alex or Nick to ask us more questions or to provide updates. We tried to limit Mackenzie's exposure to the drama as much as possible, but some questions were necessary.

A few hours before the FBI agents were going to drop us at the airport so we could fly to Austin, Alex and Nick gave me a brief update while Mackenzie swam in the indoor pool.

"We got the motherlode on Joseph," Nick said, pulling out a pack of gum. He offered me one, but I held up a hand.

"Hey, Ozzie, watch this." Mackenzie had her hands on the side of the pool, her knees tucked against her chest. She pushed off with everything she had and, floating on her back, essentially executed a backstroke start. I smiled and clapped for her when she came up for air. She smiled and went back to playing.

I turned back to Nick and Alex.

"His full name is Joseph Singler. Lived in his parents' home in East Lansing, Michigan, and worked as a part-time plumber," Nick said, chewing on his gum.

"How did—"

"It gets better, or worse," Nick said, glancing at Alex, who picked up the story.

"At the home, agents found a mound of research on Camp Israel, Malachi, a.k.a. Eldridge Kaufman, and his group. They even found emails and letters from Kaufman."

I leaned my forearms on the table just as Mackenzie jumped into the pool, sending drops of water on all of us.

"How was that? Was that a big splash?" she asked when she came up for air, wiping her hair out of her face.

"I give it a nine," Nick said with a smile.

"How about you, Ozzie?"

"Ten all the way."

"But I can do better. Just watch."

Mackenzie jumped in one more time, then became distracted and started humming and swimming on her own.

Alex chimed in. "We've been working with authorities at the prison to see if Kaufman was corresponding with Joseph. From all indications, it appears that a guard who'd gotten to know Kaufman was *pretending* to be Kaufman. He intercepted Joseph's letters, and he was the one writing or emailing back to Joseph."

"Are you guys certain Kaufman wasn't involved?"

Alex didn't respond; she just tilted her head.

"That's her way of saying she's not a hundred percent convinced," Nick said. "They've charged the guard, and the investigation continues into Kaufman. Not that he has anything to lose at this point."

Alex and Nick went on to share with me that they found a log of followers on Joseph's computer, as well as ongoing communication with players in this scheme. Gwen was the key cog in this whole conspiracy. She was sent to Hawaii to befriend Denise. She doctored the accounting books to make it seem like there was a money-laundering scheme going on at Palm Dreams Development, planted the *yakuza* angle in Denise's mind, and had the threatening note sent to her.

"But what about the two guys with nunchucks?" I asked. "They weren't from the *yakuza*?"

"Hired contractors. All to test you like you've never been tested before," Nick said.

I nodded, thinking about what they'd done to Denise. "Did you say they found a grave near the campsite?"

The agents glanced at each other. "DNA analysis is just starting at Quantico."

"No theories?" I asked.

A slight pause. Then Nick said, "We think Joseph was trying to find a blood relative of Kaufman who could withstand all of their tests. Whenever their test subjects failed, he killed them."

Part of me wanted to ponder this notion that I was related to Kaufman. From there, I could see myself obsessing over the identity of my mother. But I just didn't want to go there.

We stood up and waited for Mackenzie to get out of the pool and dry herself off. She insisted on two more cannonballs.

I put my arm around Alex as we watched. "I can't tell you how much I appreciate everything you've done for us."

"Anytime," she said with a wink.

"Planning a trip to Texas any time soon?"

Nick interjected with, "I might drag Alex and her family down with me when I go visit Stan in San Antonio."

"If you do, please let me know. Austin, if you remember from college, is still a pretty cool place."

"Just enjoy your new daughter," Alex said, smacking me on my back. "She needs you now more than ever."

We hugged. "Get back to your own kids," I said. "And tell them they have one tough mother."

"Oh, I've heard that before, but usually it ends with fu—"

I quickly raised my hand as Mackenzie walked up, toweling herself off. "It's okay, I've heard people cuss before. Even the F word."

I could only hope that was the worst of what she'd witnessed in her young life—a few cuss words. Regardless, it was time for me to step up and be the parent she needed. I was ready for the challenge.

Forty-Nine

Three weeks later

The setting sun glimmered off Lady Bird Lake. Mackenzie and I sat on a small cliff in Laguna Gloria, a fourteen-acre outdoor art-sculpture park. We'd just finished looking at the last of the pieces, something called "Canopy Tower," which was made of Ipe wood, rope, steel, and wire and stood almost sixteen feet tall. Like most of the sculptures, it was odd, but interesting. Kind of like Austin.

Texas Child Protective Services, under heavy guidance from the FBI, had given me temporary custody of Mackenzie while they determined if any relatives were living and wanted to claim her. They wouldn't have a chance at getting her, Alex assured me. I just had to wait out the bureaucracy. Mackenzie was fine with the arrangement.

It was still winter, but the temperatures were in the mid-fifties. Mackenzie kicked her feet every few seconds and stared at the water. She appeared lost in her thoughts. She'd been in that state for most of the last three weeks. I hadn't seen much of the little girl Denise had described. I knew she'd been through a lot. I'd taken her to a handful of therapy sessions. The doctor told me after the last one that I just had to be patient.

And so I was.

"You can't surf in that water, can you?" she asked.

"Nope. It's a lake. Nothing like the Pacific Ocean." I knew she was thinking about her life back in Hawaii.

I'd talked to Keo on the Big Island. He was ecstatic about me finding Mackenzie. He invited us to come back whenever we wanted. He said he'd make sure his buddy would put us up in the Four Seasons. I told him I'd hold him to that.

I'd also spoken to Brook, and she was just as happy for me, for us. She'd stopped by earlier in the week, when we were moving into my new pad, which happened to be one block from Tito's.

Nicole had called me the day I got back into town. "Your daughter is like family to me, Ozzie. Both of you need to move in. Come back home, baby."

It was tempting on so many levels. Just having another female around would be nice on a daily basis, especially since I was a complete rookie at this father-daughter thing. And even on the phone, I could feel that magnetic tug at my heart. But just as quickly, I felt another pull for the other girl in my life. Mackenzie. The last thing she needed was me and Nicole trying to sort out our issues—and despite Nicole's comments saying the opposite, I knew we had plenty to sort through. I said thanks and that we just needed to take it slow. Mackenzie and I still had some getting-to-know-you stuff to do.

Had I used Mackenzie as an excuse? Maybe. But it was a good one.

I still needed to introduce Mackenzie to my mom and her new girlfriend—if she was even still in the picture—and my brother, Tobin. He might end up being a pretty cool uncle. Being with Mackenzie in Austin reminded me how much I missed my dad, my adoptive dad. Not the lunatic bio dad, but the man who had raised me. I could picture how much joy he would have gotten out of Mackenzie, and vice versa.

"Hey," Mackenzie said. "You know, up until now, I've been calling you Ozzie."

"I know. That's okay by me. I usually respond to that name."

"Well, I've been thinking about Mom and stuff. She and I had a little talk last night. She said it would be good for me to go ahead and call you Dad. You cool with that?"

"Yeah, I'm cool with that."

My phone buzzed for about the hundredth time since we'd sat down. I pulled it out of my pocket, but she snatched it from my hand.

"This is the same guy who's been texting you for the last few weeks. You need to call him back."

"I will. But you're more important right now."

A single nod. "Okay. I get it. But didn't you say you were going to become a private investigator?"

"I've been thinking about it."

"Okay. Well, we can't eat on my good looks alone." She arched an eyebrow, then grinned in that playful way I'd seen in her picture. "It's time to get to work."

She hopped up, took a few steps, and waved me on. "Let's go, Dad. You can call this guy from the car, okay?"

I knew instantly that I had my hands full. "You're the boss, sweetie."

I climbed to my feet—I could feel that hitch in my step from my hip injury. She talked the entire way back to the car.

I'd found my jewel. And she was as perfect as they came.

Next In The Redemption Thriller Series - ON The Rocks

Her allure is undeniable. But is it also toxic?

Ozzie is determined to make this PI gig work, but only on his terms. And then Rosie shows up. She's desperate to get dirt on her powerful, womanizing husband and move on. Ozzie knows he has a soft spot for those who've been taken advantage of.

A case of spousal cheating turns deadly. Who is the culprit? More importantly, who was the intended victim?

Even with Ozzie's heart still drawn to Nicole, he knows he can't turn his back on the woman who needs him most. He just needs a little time to pull the pieces together.

And then all hell breaks loose.

Another murder...this one more personal than the first. Ozzie can't make sense of any of it. The lies, the cheating all blur together. He's stuck in the middle of this twisted storm, unable to find the truth, losing trust in his ability to deny his desires.

Can a life of abuse justify a seduction of greed? And can Ozzie somehow uncover the root of the conspiracy before more lives are lost?

Who will be the last woman standing?

ON The Rocks is the third Ozzie Novak Thriller (Redemption Thriller Series #15). An excerpt follows.

Excerpt from ON THE ROCKS (Book 3)

One

Crouching under a car that was jacked up on a lift, I hobbled over a spare tire and almost face-planted on the concrete floor. And this was all just to get from my office at the northeast corner of Gartner Automotive to the other side of the garage.

I was beginning to wonder if I should just go with the flow and call my new business venture "Grease Monkey Investigative Services."

I heard a laugh—more like the braying of a donkey—and turned to see Steve Gartner, owner of the repair shop, approaching me. Wiping his filthy hands on a shop towel, he said, "Nice moves, Ozzie."

"Very funny. I'm gonna kill myself walking through here one of these days. You got some tissues?"

"Don't tell me—you got a lady crying in your office, right?" He snapped his fingers. "I know I'm right. And she wants you to catch her evil, cheating husband in the act of *adul-ter-y*. Am I right?"

I rolled my eyes. As much as I tried to avoid them, that was pretty much *the only* clientele who entered the PI office on the other side of the repair shop. I wiggled my fingers at him. "Tissues?"

"Yeah, yeah. Let me look." We walked into his office, and he began rummaging around. The space was filled with miscellaneous tools, car parts, magazines, receipts, food containers, notepads. Oh, and let's not forget Steve's creepy stuffed cat named Hermit. A tissue was probably the *only* thing Steve *didn't* have in his office.

Just like his brother, Ray.

Ray, of Ray Gartner Private Investigation Services, had skipped town a few weeks back after being beaten to a pulp—including having half his ear bitten off. Ray had been doing some work for me at the time and believed there was only one option for him to stay alive. He was running for the border, going off the grid forever. He'd suggested I do the same. I had no intention of leaving my hometown of Austin. He told me I was nuts, handed me the keys to his office, and said I could have it all.

"All" was a PI business whose clientele seemed to have captured the market for cheating husbands and wives. Not my specialty—I was a lawyer by trade—but my life had changed so much in such a short amount of time…well, this PI business was something I was seriously considering. Though not without much trepidation.

"Got to have some tissues in here somewhere." *Rummage, rummage, rummage.* "So, how's things going?"

I wasn't in the mood to carry on a conversation. Steve was a good guy, but he could be annoying as hell at times. Plus, the mix of sweat, grime, dust, and motor oil was getting to me. Looking back out over the garage space, I nestled my nose in the crook of my arm.

"Cat got your tongue, Ozzie?" He did that braying noise again.

I didn't even bother to look. I knew he was pointing at that damn stuffed cat.

Ever since I'd returned from my own sabbatical—which involved a harried race across the country to locate a daughter I never knew I had—Steve had been cracking jokes, sometimes at my expense. It was all in fun, though. He was just happy that someone was around to handle the constant requests for Ray's services.

"Okay, so, no tissues?"

"Let me check one more place." He opened the bottom drawer of a rusty filing cabinet. "Aha! I knew I had some." He pulled out a roll of toilet paper, tossing it in my direction.

My client would be so impressed.

Two

"Sorry about that." I tore off four sheets of toilet paper and handed them to the somber woman sitting in front of the desk that I could barely get to. By pure luck, I managed to get to the chair behind my desk without tripping or knocking over something.

Rosie Alvarado didn't seem thrown off by the toilet paper, which shocked the hell out of me. Instead, she grabbed the wad and honked as she blew her nose. I held back a smirk, only because it was the last thing I'd expected. She was petite, and her honk was…well, larger than petite.

She dropped her hands to her lap. "I'm not sure where I left off." She sighed as though it was her last breath. Her despair was obvious.

I could only nod. Which was of no help whatsoever. Despite her apparent despair, she was lovely. Of course, I couldn't put her in the same league as Nicole, who was, at least in my mind, a ten—philanderer be damned.

I don't know what it was exactly about this woman; she didn't come across as "aware" of her beauty. She didn't flaunt it, snap it. But the aura coming off her was impossible not to notice.

I was married—more or less—but I wasn't blind. Partially deaf, yes, but not blind. And I still had my other senses. My instincts, for one.

I'd grown weary of sitting in this same office, hearing spouses tell me all about the lies, the cheating, the excuses, the blame game. And the hate. It was the hate that made me cringe. I'd been living it myself recently. Hearing another version of the same story was like having acid reflux—it just burned more on the second time down. But there was something different about Rosie.

I finally prompted her. "Your husband, Earl. He's been less attentive than usual, which wasn't much to begin with, and you've been thinking about that. You remembered some, uh, signs, or things you thought might be signs."

She lowered her eyelids and shrugged. "More a sense than anything." A pause and then a sputtering breath. "A woman knows!" She put her head in her hands and wept.

I hated to see her, anyone, go through this turmoil. And it only stirred my emotions that much more. The last thing I wanted was to think of Nicole and what she'd done to me, our marriage.

Rosie Alvarado had to be no more than thirty, just a couple of years north of my age. Her husband, from what I'd seen from his image plastered on the large billboards with his namesake business, Earl's Truck Stop, had to be pushing seventy, if not more. I put my fingers on my tablet keyboard and thought about typing in a couple of notes. The only words that came to mind—and I'm not exactly proud of this—were "sugar daddy" and "gold digger."

Yet, she seemed nothing like that.

How had she come to meet and marry Earl? *Stranger things have happened, I suppose.*

"I'm sure this is tough for you, Rosie. Whenever you're ready, I'm here to listen." There. I'd given my standard Ozzie Novak response, the one I'd uttered dozens of times during my life as an attorney working for Novak and Novak. No, I wasn't rich. The firm had been dissolved, and I eventually realized I wasn't fond of the profession anyway. In many respects, my entire life needed a reboot. My incredible newfound daughter, Mackenzie, was now my top priority. But I had to pay the bills, particularly since we lived separately from my wife, Nicole—*the one who'd trashed our marriage*. Okay, I knew I wasn't a perfect person, probably had my own set of issues, but she'd been my rock for so long. Until she wasn't.

I almost wanted to hold up a hand to Rosie and spend about twenty seconds summarizing her story, just so I wouldn't be forced to listen to every granular detail. But then she looked up at me with her pleading chocolate eyes: "Will you help me?"

Well, how could I say no to that? But I held back. "You're going to have to tell me more, Rosie. I know it's hard, but it's not really a matter of *if* I want to help you, but *can* I help you."

"Yes, of course." She swallowed hard. "Earl saved me from an abusive relationship."

"How so?"

"Can we— Is it important that I go into every single detail?"

It wasn't. Not yet.

Leaning my elbows on the desk, I said, "No, of course not. I only need information that will help you accomplish…to help you move on."

She swallowed and became silent, her eyes falling into a catatonic state. She had this mole on the side of her cheek, which was adorable.

"Rosie, you okay? Can I get you—" I stopped short. What the hell was I thinking? I had no beverages to offer her. This office needed a serious facelift. "So, Rosie, what exactly do you want me to do?"

She cleared her throat. "My ex, Billy, was abusive...in many ways. He always told me how stupid I was." She was focused on this Billy person for some reason. I figured trauma reared its ugly head in many ways.

"Sounds like a real asshole."

She looked up at me, her eyes filled with tears. She giggled and then covered her mouth. "Not funny, but it is. Yes, he was an asshole, Mr. Novak. But I apologize. I seem to be dwelling on things from the past, and I'm not being very helpful as a result. May I start again?"

"Of course, and please know, I understand. Go on." Helpful Ozzie.

She coughed into her hand and then pursed her lips. "Okay, so when I met Earl, I was in the hospitality industry."

Running my fingers through my thick blond hair, I could feel my brow furrow. *Hospitality industry?* I was almost afraid to ask. No way this heartbroken woman could be...like, an escort? I swiveled my chair around as I considered her words. In doing so, I spotted a piece of paper taped to the lone filing cabinet. It was a sketch that Mackenzie had drawn. And it wasn't your typical fourth-grader drawing. She had serious skills. This was a simple— her term, not mine—sketch of a dog jumping into a lake. Mackenzie loved the water, just like her father—me. I treasured every single one of those similarities between us, and even the dissimilarities too. Those would remind me of her late mother and of all the ancestors behind us, whose genes contributed to that unique little person who was my daughter.

As I swung my chair back around to face Rosie, I accidentally kicked over a two-foot stack of old magazines—all *Sports Illustrated Swimsuit* issues. I bent down, wrestled them back into a messy pile, and then sat up straight in the chair again.

Focus, Oz. "So, you work for a hotel, or what exactly?"

"Food services." She curled a lock of her hair around her ear. "Okay, basically, I was a waitress." Her olive skin became flush.

I nodded. "Nothing wrong with that."

"No, there is not." She lifted her chin. "I come from a humble family. We didn't have much, other than our pride and support of each other. I am their prize child, the one most likely to succeed. And I have done nothing but fail." She dropped her head.

My protective nature kicked in. "Way too hard on yourself, Rosie. We make choices, though some are made for us. Don't beat yourself up."

She laughed with a nod of her head. "I suppose. Anyway, I'm ready to get my life back. Even if I end up being a waitress again. My family has been in the serving business for a long time, many generations. No shame in that." She glimpsed at me beneath the cover of her incredibly long lashes. Natural, I was certain. That was why she seemed so different. She was authentic, with some actual depth.

"No shame in that at all," I agreed emphatically. "So, you believe Earl has been cheating on you. You want me to find out if that's true, so you can make some decisions and forge a better life. Does that sum it up?"

She smiled. I stopped blinking for a moment. That damn smile was so wide it crossed her entire face.

She said, "Yes, that's where I'm at right now." She sighed, but this one sounded more like relief. "Finally. I have some ideas about how to do this…"

I was all ears, as much as I could be.

Three

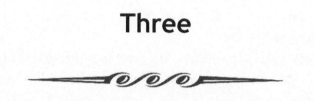

Rosie walked back into the office, waving a hand in front of her face, wrinkling her nose. It was cute.

"Sorry about the restrooms. The lug-heads," I said, waving a hand toward the shop area, "have the bathroom habits of a toddler."

She sat in the chair, crossed her legs. Her black-and-white print dress had this little slit up the side. "Thank you for giving me a minute to myself."

"No problem. I know you're struggling with many difficult memories right now." I sat up in my old chair. It whined like it was about to croak.

She looked down and then pushed a lock of her hair to the side. It was black and luminous, yet just thrown together on top of her head, as if it were held in place by some gravity-defying force. I could see she was trying to find the right words to say. I picked up a rubber band and twisted it around my finger. When I glanced up at her, the rubber band shot out of my hand, smacking the window. She flinched.

Damn, her nerves were raw.

"Sorry about that." I scooted around the desk and found the rubber band dangling on the corner of a Longhorn window sticker.

I snatched it up and shuffled my way back to my chair. "Everything in Austin is all about the university. I'm sure that will never change." I forced out a chuckle.

She tried to smile, but it never made it to her eyes.

"I went to school there for a couple of years, until…well, let's just say I had a personality conflict with one of my professors."

A long nod by me.

"Copeland," she said, as if she were speaking to herself.

I couldn't hear worth a damn, but I could read lips. And that was the name she'd uttered. Dr. Garrett Copeland had been my nemesis when I was a sophomore at the University of Texas. He made it his life's mission to give me grief three times a week at eight a.m. He reveled in it. I wasn't his only target. He seemed to loathe most young people who dared walk into his classroom. Well, anyone who didn't have an hourglass figure. I could still recall his derisive comments about…everything.

"Did you take a class with Dr. Copeland?"

Her eyes fluttered like the wings of frantic bird. "I, uh…" She looked anxious.

"I didn't mean to upset you."

"No, I…" She swallowed, let out a gasp.

"What is it, Rosie?'

"It's…" She put a trembling hand to her face. Something had triggered a painful memory. "I don't mean to pry, but if it helps…"

She opened her lips and closed them, her eyes searching for a safe spot on the floor. Then, she looked up. Her dark eyes were glassy. She held my gaze for a second. I didn't turn away, but I wasn't sure whether to press her further.

"It was the day my life changed forever. Changed who I was, who I'd be…" Her breathing flickered, but there were no tears. I stayed silent, wondering if she'd share more. Part of me hoping she would, part of me hoping she wouldn't.

Finally, I couldn't help myself. I had to ask. "Rosie, what happened to you?"

"He..." Another swallow. "He raped me. He and two of his teaching assistants gang-raped me."

I could feel blood drain from my head.

John W. Mefford Bibliography

The Ozzie Novak Thrillers
ON EDGE (Book 1)
GAME ON (Book 2)
ON THE ROCKS (Book 3)
SHAME ON YOU (Book 4)
ON FIRE (Book 5)
ON THE RUN (Book 6)

The Alex Troutt Thrillers
AT BAY (Book 1)
AT LARGE (Book 2)
AT ONCE (Book 3)
AT DAWN (Book 4)
AT DUSK (Book 5)
AT LAST (Book 6)
AT STAKE (Book 7)
AT ANY COST (Book 8
BACK AT YOU (Book 9)
AT EVERY TURN (Book 10)
AT DEATH'S DOOR (Book 11)
AT FULL TILT (Book 12)

The Ivy Nash Thrillers
IN DEFIANCE (Book 1)
IN PURSUIT (Book 2)
IN DOUBT (Book 3)

BREAK IN (Book 4)
IN CONTROL (Book 5)
IN THE END (Book 6)

The Ball & Chain Thrillers
MERCY (Book 1)
FEAR (Book 2)
BURY (Book 3)
LURE (Book 4)
PREY (Book 5)
VANISH (Book 6)
ESCAPE (Book 7)

The Booker Series
BOOKER – Streets of Mayhem (Volume 1)
BOOKER – Tap That (Volume 2)
BOOKER – Hate City (Volume 3)
BOOKER – Blood Ring (Volume 4)
BOOKER – No Más (Volume 5)
BOOKER – Dead Heat (Volume 6)

The Greed Series
FATAL GREED (Greed Series #1)
LETHAL GREED (Greed Series #2)
WICKED GREED (Greed Series #3)
GREED MANIFESTO (Greed Series #4)

To stay updated on John's latest releases, visit:
JohnWMefford.com

Made in the USA
Coppell, TX
11 August 2020